EMERALD-SILK
INTRIGUE

EMERALD-SILK INTRIGUE

A Romance

by

William Maltese

Writing as "Willa Lambert"

The Borgo Press
An Imprint of Wildside Press

MMVII

SECOND EDITION

1

Jessica Miller cringed as she heard Jeff Billings shout, "What skeletons are you so intent upon keeping in the family closets?"

Roman Whyte ignored the words as he slammed the limousine door and signaled his driver to leave. The Church members seemed mezmerized by the proceedings.

She'd never dreamed when she offered to show Jeff the way to the Bangkok chapel this morning that he was coming solely to interrogate Roman. He'd mentioned that he wrote unauthorized biographies, but she had no idea that Roman was his quarry. She'd think twice and quell her missionary spirit before she ever again helped a stranger find the church.

Feeling the flush of embarrassment tinge her face, she decided to escape before Jeff wondered where the ever-so-helpful Jessica had gotten off to. Turning to her friend

Nora Spencer, Jessica said quickly, "It's good to see you again. I'll give you a ring during the week, and maybe we can get together while I'm here." Hardly waiting for her reply, Jessica hurried down the steps and melted into the crowd, anxious to get away from the curious stares of the members.

Since Sunday was just another workday to the Buddhists in Bangkok, she needed only to take a few steps down the road in order to become engulfed within a concealing maze that consisted of goods and services, plus the people who bought and sold them.

She quickly sidestepped a stand that overflowed with exotic durians, jackfruits and other succulent edibles that she still couldn't identify in their entirety. Looking back to make sure no one had followed her, she threaded her way through a labyrinth of beggars, shopkeepers, raggedy children, and well-dressed Thais, hoping she blended in. Without slowing down, she detoured around an old woman who sold a soupy mixture of vegetables and noodles out of a sharp-edged jerrican propped on bricks in the middle of the sidewalk. Nearby, another old woman carefully poured tannin-colored tea from a rusted pot, each time being sure to retrieve her one chipped cup when it was emptied by a customer.

Several blocks later, certain she was free, Jessica slowed down and contemplated the route to her hotel. All of a sudden her intuition warned her that she was being followed. A hasty glance over her shoulder confirmed that the stranger she now regretted helping was among the tapestry of moving bodies behind her.

To what possible purpose did he give chase? Surely he wasn't such a glutton for punishment that he'd seek her out just to hear her indignation at being used to further his schemes. His tousled hair would stand up in spikes like the tortured coiffures of punkers Jessica had seen on a London street corner, if she gave vent to her feelings.

On the other hand, maybe he wasn't following her at all. Why should he, after all she'd served her purpose. Coincidence may have had them headed in the same direction. If so, it would be easy enough to escape him. She turned the next corner and walked even faster.

Convinced she'd succeeded in avoiding what would have been an uncomfortable situation, Jessica was genuinely startled when she felt her arm suddenly grasped from behind. She was anything but pleased to find the offending hand belonged to Jeff, and her expression must have relayed that message, because he immediately removed his grip, if not the sensation it had mysteriously created.

Jessica couldn't believe she'd actually been charmed by this man in The Oriental Hotel lobby this morning.

"I don't like the scene you caused at the church," she said. Buffeted there, like a piece of flotsam in the stream of swiftly flowing pedestrian traffic, was suddenly as good a place as any to set him straight.

She refused to be won over by his good looks, even if they were enhanced by a faint pursing of his lips and by a certain disconcerting something in his brown eyes. The latter reminded her of someone's favorite horse uncertain as to why its owner's riding crop had been laid on a sweaty flank too hard. Well, Jessica wasn't going to be taken in by any of it a second time.

"Deny you used me to get to Roman Whyte, Mr. Billings!"

"I thought we agreed you'd call me Jeff?" he parried and blinked sooty eyelashes so thick, long, and black that more than one of Jessica's models would die for them. Jessica wouldn't have turned them down herself. Turning down the man who owned them was another thing altogether, her resolve only confirmed when he added with perturbing familiarity, "And I call you Jessica, right?"

How wrong he was!

"I think, under the circumstances, we should revert to our original Mr. Billings-Miss Miller format," Jessica said and resumed walking.

Unfortunately, her hint was apparently too subtle for him to follow, because he joined her in her zigzag within the unending mixture of people and goods-for-sale. Their swift pace stirred otherwise stale air to waft the exotic smells of the orient: pungent garlic, aromatic cardamon, distinctive tumeric, and savory lemon grass. With a start, Jessica realized the latter was pleasantly emanating from Jeff, probably the aftermath of an early-morning splash of citrus-based after-shave or cologne.

She flashed him a sideways glance and decided his handsomeness fit right into this city of colors too vibrant; noises too loud; weather too hot; rain, when it came, too abundant; and food too spicy, too sweet, or too sour. For Jessica, who preferred to savor things individually, and at leisure, Bangkok was an assault on the senses, and Jeff's too-good looks were part of the assault team.

"How could you?" she asked when his apology wasn't forthcoming. There was no doubt in her mind that his apology was warranted and necessary. "You only had one reason for going to church, didn't you?" she said. "To corner Roman Whyte!"

She turned left on Ratchawong, which, had she turned right, would be Sua Pa Road. The change of street names, mid-block, was one of the most confusing aspects of the city, and it was the one Jeff had successfully used earlier to get Jessica to feel sympathy for a first-timer to Bangkok who wanted to visit a local Latter-day Saint meeting but was having trouble finding it.

Jessica had been here enough times to know where she was usually headed—this time toward the distant Chao Phraya River where she hoped for a quick water taxi to her hotel. Preferably *not* with Jeff in tow.

An unanticipated surge of oncoming foot traffic squeezed her off the narrow sidewalk. It was just her distorted brand of luck to have it be Jeff who kept her from losing her balance in the path of a tuk tuk, one of the three-wheeled tricycles that pulled passengers rickshaw-fashion through traffic-clogged streets. He took hold in order to steady her.

"Thanks," Jessica breathed, a little light-headed from her near miss. Granted, a tuk tuk wasn't a two-ton truck, but she knew from past experience, and had a small scar on her left leg to prove it, that a collision with one wasn't to be eagerly endured.

This time, she didn't insist Jeff remove his hand from her arm until it was embarrassingly obvious it had remained far too long.

"How about if we decelerate to a slow trot?" Jeff suggested and rubbed the fingers of his recently free hand across his lips as if he were savoring what remained of her touch. "Or is one of us going to a fire?"

"I don't know about you, Mr. Billings. . ."

"Jeff," he insisted.

"I don't know about you, Mr. Billings," Jessica stubbornly persisted, "but I came to Bangkok to work."

"On Sunday?" he chided, as if he were the good Mormon and Jessica the errant gentile to be proselyted, not vice versa. "Come on, and let me buy you lunch. It's the least I can do for whatever trouble I've caused you."

Jessica glanced around and expected to see Roman glaring at her.

"Do you *really* know the potential problems you could have caused me?" Jessica asked. She stopped walking to emphasize her question, and they once again became an island in a stream of pedestrians that obligingly opened, then closed around them.

"You mean problems with Roman Whyte?" he ventured.

"Who else?" Jessica responded, incredulous that he could act so innocent. "You came up to me in the hotel lobby this morning and asked to go along with me to services at my church, and an altercation with Roman Whyte on the front steps is how you repay me for being helpful, Mr. Billings."

"Jeff," he tried once again. "Now how about lunch?"

"Thanks for the invitation, but no thanks," she decided. She was hungry, all right, but she could eat back at her hotel—alone. There was grilled *kapong* fish on the Normandie Room lunch menu that would fit her needs nicely.

"Don't you think you're prematurely overreacting to how Roman is going to take all of this, especially as I have all intentions of explaining to him that you were only playing Good Samaritan?" Jeff asked with a self-congratulatory smile.

"Roman knows me well enough to realize I would have had to be an unsuspecting dupe to be involved in any of this," Jessica assured. "However, your offer is appreciated, since you could hardly be expected to know he wouldn't need you to verify my innocence." Then again, it was Jeff's having never been able to know for sure how Roman would react to Jessica's part in all of this that kept her anger from cooling. What if Jessica hadn't been able to count so surely upon Roman's understanding? An alienated Roman could make her life difficult from a business standpoint. Whyte Silk Consortium wasn't the only wholesale outlet for Thai silk in the country, but it provided the irrefutable guarantees of workmanship and quality that Jessica and her customers had come to expect as their right. Roman's people had worked with Jessica enough to know what she wanted and expected, and vice versa. All of which made her buying silk for her dress designs far less hassle than it could be.

"And since it's the thought that counts, why not agree to lunch with me as your gracious way of saying you at least appreciate my good intentions?" Jeff brazenly suggested, obviously unaware of the shift in Jessica's line of reasoning.

"The road to hell is paved with good intentions, and sometimes mere intentions are not nearly agood enough apology," she told him with undeniable satisfaction.

"According to the guide book, I can offer French, Hungarian, Austrian, German, Italian, English, Swiss, Scandinavian, American, and, of course, Thai cuisine, all within easy access from this very spot," he rambled on, as if he didn't know an out-and-out refusal when it hit him on the head. "The tourist trade has been going great guns in Thailand since back when the country was known as Siam, and there's a plethora of western-style restaurants, three of which have made a recent 'Asian Wall Street Journal' list of the ten best in the whole Far East."

No matter the harmless fantasies Jessica entertained earlier that day when she'd first been approached by this attractive man in need of a seemingly harmless favor, those idle daydreams had vanished when Jeff confronted Roman.

"How about if we subscribe to the die-hard tradition of when in Rome do as the Romans?" Jeff suggested.

Jessica thought if anyone was die-hard, it was Jeff Billings. Besides, his unfortunate reference to "Romans" was an ill-timed play on words that only emphasized it was Roman Whyte, waiting somewhere off in the wings, who made Jessica see Jeff as definitely *persona non grata.* Not that Jeff got the connection, as was evidenced by his, "There's a good Thai restaurant right up this very block."

"Look, I really don't want to be of any further help to you," Jessica said. "Roman will understand how you might have conned me into helping you once, but he won't understand any continuation of our socializing now when your intentions are clear. And I can't say I'd blame him."

Jeff had the unabashed temerity to take her hand, and had she even vaguely suspected his handhold as anything more than the easiest way for any two people to maneuver the Bangkok crowds in unison, she would have freed her hand. As it was, she tried a time or two to wrench free, then allowed herself to be guided through the gauntlet of people and things that stood between them and the restaurant he had obviously selected for them. *Then,* she pulled free and rubbed her fingers as if the sensations turned loose within them were the total result of his firm grip having cut off her circulation.

"*Laow Ped*?" she read from the calligraphic neon sign that would have been bright pink if turned on. "Doesn't that roughly translate 'Spicy Whiskey'?" She grimaced.

"Whatever its name, don't hold it against it," he pleaded. "The food is delicious. Trust me."

Trust him? She'd trusted him earlier, and where had it gotten her? The center of a scene in front of the chapel. However, she had gone this far, so she went farther and let a waiter show them to a back booth. Two Thai families, complete with well-mannered children, occupied a couple of the other booths and gave the place an air of respectability that had been lacking in the neon sign outside.

Jessica decided the inside lighting, dim as it was, was what made Jeff look so good, and she hoped it did the same for her. On the other hand, he hadn't looked all that bad in broad daylight, either. There was something horribly trite about tall, dark, and handsome, but it certainly seemed to fit here. Not that it was something she couldn't handle. There were plenty of attractive men in the fashion business.

"It's not as if I arrived in Bangkok with a preconceived notion of enlisting your help in getting to Roman," Jeff argued. "I merely heard that Roman was a regular church-goer, whenever he was in Bangkok, and I asked the hotel concierge for transportation to the chapel in question. He suggested it might behoove me to get in touch with you, since you're another regular church-goer, whenever you're in Bangkok. How was I to know you not only knew Roman but he'd possibly blame you for my being there?"

"I would expect a well-known author like yourself to put one and two together, and come up with three," she retorted. "One, I'm a Mormon in Thailand to buy silk. Two, Roman is a Mormon in Thailand and the majority stockholder in Whyte Silk Consortium, Limited. Equals three, Roman and I might know each other from Bangkok, church, business, or any two or three of the above."

"Yes, but I'm concentrating on Roman's uncle, not on Roman," Jeff said. "Had you had any kind of close relationship with the late Powell Whyte, the chances are good I would have known about it. Then, you might conceivably argue successfully that it wasn't just my innocent need for someone familiar with the lay of the land that prompted me to call upon you for assistance in maneuvering Bangkok streets."

The waiter returned for their orders. Jessica, who had spent the last few minutes with her menu propped open in front of her, hadn't even glanced at the food selection. "You go ahead," she instructed Jeff, finally giving the extensive list a once-over. Her eyes automatically sorted out the dishes made familiar by her previous visits to the city: a whole range of beef, pork, chicken, or seafood dishes *gang pet*, meaning with hot curry; *kao pat*, meaning with fried rice; *homok*, meaning in a paste of shrimp, chillies, onions, garlic, coconut milk, soy sauce, egg, and finely sliced raw fish.

"*Tom yam*," Jeff ordered, and Jessica would have ordered the same, but such "salad soups," in the past, had usually proved a trifle too sour for her tastes.

"*Gaeng chud*," she said instead. It was a similar but more ordinary vegetable soup flavored with coriander which was popular in Thailand.

She surrendered her menu, settled back, and wondered if the perverse pleasure she could still take in Jeff's company had something to do with his being a fellow American in a land that, despite Jessica's several visits to it, remained exotically alien. Granted, her church connections had made her introduction less complicated than it might have been, but there was no denying there was still something about the place that made it difficult for westerners to assimilate entirely.

"So, how many of your other biographies were as

unauthorized as this one?" she asked and decided he couldn't be as surprised by her instinctive probe as he looked. If Roman hadn't been pleased to see him, and he hadn't been, it followed the same could be said for a lot of the other people Jeff had interviewed during his writing career. "Three previous books, is it? One on Howard Caskill who had more in common with the late Howard Hughes than first names: both having made fortunes, movies, headlines, and enemies; both having died in seclusion. One on Gregory Wentlake, a silent partner of Cecil Rhodes; Gregory having managed a good many political and business machinations without the publicity that attended his more theatrical partner's each and every move. One on Terrence—who?"

"McAter," Jeff filled in for her; Terrence McAter the only one of the three subjects about whom Jessica had known nothing before Jeff had given her a rundown on his writing credentials on their way to church that morning. Not that the superficial knowledge she did have of the other two was because of any past exposure to Jeff's tomes. Most of Jessica's reading was still confined to the fashion and merchandising industries: a habit developed during her long years of survival in the dog-eat-dog world of New York fashion, and a habit hard to break. The monthly check she'd needed to pay for the nursing care of her mother had been another good incentive to keep all of Jessica's activities pretty much telescoped on business.

"McAter was in munitions," she finally remembered.

"Right," Jeff concurred and opened the bottle of water the waiter brought them.

The water reminded Jessica of her first "Welcome to Bangkok" brochure in which a section, "Most Often Asked Questions," queried: "Is the tap water potable?" The answer had been a resounding "NO!" A detailed account of the city's primitive open-air sewers had followed, along with explanations of pollutant seepage into the water table. Jessica had been converted to bottled water, right then and there. She hadn't wavered since, despite more than one long-time resident who always argued with conviction that the local water was excellent, the bad-mouthing of it was a conspiracy of greedy advertisers of bottled water anxious to bilk foreigners out of even more tourist dollars.

"So, will you graciously join me in a toast to my *unauthorized* biography number four?" Jeff asked, raising his glass.

"Only so long as it doesn't complicate my life any further," Jessica qualified, hoisting her glass and tapping it to Jeff's. The resulting chime of crystal was pleasantly on key.

"Fair enough," Jeff conceded and took a sip. His smile showed a double row of white teeth so seemingly perfect that Jessica was sure they were capped. As for his perfect dimple, revealed by his perfect smile, as registered on his too-perfect face, Jessica wondered how any one man could have so lucked out in the looks department; it hardly seemed fair. Then again, maybe Jeff didn't look all that fantastic to someone who didn't have the admitted bias Jessica had for dark-complexioned men. Someone else might well complain that Jeff was too swarthy, his hair too dark, his eyes too brown. Someone really critical would point to the small black mole almost concealed by the hairline at Jeff's right temple.

"Wouldn't it be easier to write *authorized* biographies?" Jessica asked, embarrassed she might be staring. She returned her glass to the table, more at ease now that she'd spotted his mole.

"Authorized biographies are always easier," Jeff agreed. "Being greeted with open arms by friends and relatives of the subject cuts down considerably on the legwork required to ferret out some kinds of information. However — and this is a mighty big however, Jessica — family and friends have a tendency to be overly protective and guarded about those aspects of a loved one's life which usually make the most interesting reading."

"The scandal and dirt, you mean?" Jessica asked, although it wasn't really a question. She always felt guilty whenever she succumbed to temptation in grocery store check-out lines and scanned the exploitive headlines of the tabloids.

"It's always been my belief that people who make money off other people owe a general accounting to someone," Jeff said. "Too often they exist by self-made rules and regulations that have nothing whatsoever to do with the laws of the land. I'm continually appalled by how some people can get away with literal murder, while friends and relatives rally round to keep the skeletons from tumbling pell-mell out of guilt-cluttered closets. The minute people start pointing fingers and screaming about my being a no-good so-and-so out to blacken a man's good name, or about my being an agent of the Devil out to pull the wings off some angel-on-earth, I suspect a cover-up and, more often than no, it's there to find."

The food arrived, and Jessica confirmed, by tasting, that it was as delicious as it looked and smelled. She waited for Jeff to sample his before she continued their conversation.

"Roman was definitely not pleased to see you at church today," she confirmed for him. "He masked it very well, from all that I overheard, but a man in less control would have dropped you on the spot, or at least given instructions for Nikolas to do it."

"Nikolas?"

"Roman's bodyguard and chauffeur."

"Ah, the potential bone-crusher! He *was* looking at me as if he'd like to chew me alive for breakfast."

"That's the gentleman all right," Jessica admitted with a smile.

"So, I'm glad Roman has good self-control, but if I eventually make him lose it, then so be it! I have every reason to believe Roman's uncle wasn't the upstanding, lily-pure businessman, art collector, and philanthropist he's been painted, and I plan to prove it." He spooned another sample of colorful vegetable soup. "Did you know that Powell Whyte, at the time of his unexplained murder, had not one, not two, but three public relations firms on his payroll to regulate what did and didn't appear about him in the world media?"

"I'd hate to see Roman hurt by any scandal," Jessica said. She didn't add that Roman would have been more to her than merely a special friend if the magic Roman and she had hoped for hadn't eluded them. She could still marvel at how all the apparently right ingredients, including the same religion and a mutual desire for something to happen, had not supplied a marriage, let alone any they-lived-happily-ever-afters. Not that she would ever denigrate their resulting friendship, because she understood, from those who professed to know, that good friends were often more difficult to come by than husbands, though, still single at thirty-six, figured she just might have good grounds to argue the point.

"What do you think of my determination to wield my journalistic scalpel and slice through the respectability of

Powell Whyte and lay bare the possible corruption underneath?"

"I can't believe Roman is knowingly involved in anything illegal!" she said with succinct finality.

"Well, you're allowed your opinion, to be sure," Jeff said and took another swallow of soup. "On the other hand, I think even a religious person isn't above a bit of slipping and sliding now and again, when dollar signs start to dazzle."

Jessica frowned. For a moment she'd forgotten Jeff wasn't a Mormon and never had been one. He sat across from her drinking water, not liquor or wine, his conversation not once laced with a swear word. On her part she'd better be careful. Such forgetfulness would be better replaced by constant vigilance when confronted by someone as attractive and as winning as Jeff was.

"But, it's primarily Powell Whyte with whom I'm concerned," Jeff reminded her. "Roman's honesty or dishonesty applies here only as an interesting aside on how corruption can possibly be handed down, from generation to generation, as easily as any other family inheritance." He smiled his hey-I'm not-a-bad-guy smile and showed his undeniably fetching dimple. "Lucky for me, Powell Whyte never converted to Mormonism along with his nephew, right?"

"Lucky how?" Jessica asked, her spoon paused halfway to her mouth. She made a conscious effort to control a certain inexplicable something on the loose inside her. She decided she was chilling, despite the temperature and humidity.

"Oh, I don't exactly know how," Jeff procrastinated with a shrug, and Jessica knew he knew, all right. She tried to decide whether to be flattered or not.

"There are imperfect people in every religion," she said. "If every person were perfect, there'd be little point to any of us being here, would there?"

"I still remain glad I'm not about to blast *two* of 'your people' out of the water," Jeff insisted. "I mean, it's not often I have the pleasure of such attractive company, and I wouldn't want to alienate the prettiest woman in Bangkok because she thought I was anti-Mormon."

"I really must be getting back to the hotel," she said, deciding she'd had enough. With a painful slowness, so he wouldn't realize he'd spooked her, she reached for the napkin on her lap and used it to blot her lips a final time. In reality, she was disturbed that he thought she might find a man's religion enough grounds to excuse and conceal any sins.

"You'll be missing a rare treat if you pass up dessert," Jeff warned, apparently unaware of the tug-of-war in progress inside her. "The *salim* here is out of this world."

"I really must pass," Jessica persisted, although her sweet tooth cried out for the satisfaction of again tasting those thin strings of delectably sweet noodles floating in coconut milk with small chunks of ice. "I'm on a diet." She was *always* on a diet.

"Well, I'd be the last person to try and persuade you to do something to spoil your marvelous figure," Jeff said by way of obvious compliment.

"However, *you* should feel free to stay," Jessica insisted, surveying the table to make sure she left nothing behind. The last thing she wanted was Jeff knocking on her hotel door with the excuse, "You rushed off and left this at the restaurant." The less she saw of him, the better. She'd thought that after hearing Roman and Jeff at church. She still thought that now.

"I wouldn't think of staying on without you," Jeff protested. "Just give me a moment to settle the bill."

Jessica helplessly eyed the front door. Anyone would have thought she was trying to flee a life-threatening situation, although Jeff was actually acting a perfect gentleman.

"You really must let me pay my share," Jessica insisted, since it might be better if she didn't let him chalk up even minor favors. She hadn't decided if her consenting to join him for lunch constituted an adequate payment for his having pulled her out from in front of the tuk tuk. There was a distinct chance they were already irreversibly on opposite sides concerning this book of his.

"Nonsense!" Jeff objected with a do-be-serious smile. "I invited you to lunch, right? Even the most stringent arbiter of etiquette would agree I'm within my rights on this one."

"Then, thanks for the lunch," Jessica conceded reluctantly. The food had been excellent, and Jeff charming, but there had been something unsettling about the whole meal which Jessica wished she could put her finger on.

She was still tempted to make a beeline through the front door, but she opted for a trip to the ladies' room instead. Not that she had plans to use any of the meager facilities she found there except the cracked and broken mirror. She'd never quite adapted to the Oriental conclusion that a mere hole in the floor adequately sufficed for one very major bathroom convenience. Luckily, The Oriental Hotel, where she always stayed, catered to western tourists and came equipped with a complete array of European/American plumbing.

She didn't despise what she saw in the restaurant

mirror. Oh, she'd given up complaining about eyes set too far apart, a nose too thin, a chin too pointy, and lips too pouty. She could do nothing about them. And they were sufficiently offset by the warm gray color of her eyes, the striking sculpture of her high cheekbones, and the graceful Modigliani-style sweep of her neck which had drawn its share of compliments from the beauty-conscious models who wore Jessica's fashion designs down glittery runways. The rosy blush on her face was another matter entirely. She decided to blame it on the ever-present Bangkok heat and humidity rather than the edge of exciement that fluttered through her body.

"Calm down!" she told her reflection as she sprinkled eau de cologne onto a linen handkerchief and bathed her forehead, cheeks, and neck. She wouldn't have touched the water dripping to form a yellow scum on the cracked porcelain of the sink, any more than she would have touched an African puff adder. "You're not some giddy teenager on your first date. You're Jessica Miller, thirty-six, highly successful and with every chance of maintaining your position in the international world of haute couture if you just keep your purpose in mind. You're in Thailand to buy the silk you need for your next collection from Roman, which means steering clear of Jeff Billings and his book at all costs!"

Jeff waited for her by the door to the street. "Everything all right?" he asked when she reluctantly rejoined him.

"I'm fine," Jessica insisted. She wasn't quite sure that was the case, but they'd both have to take her word for it.

"You look a little flushed," Jeff decided, and Jessica wasn't pleased that he'd noticed. Even less pleasant was the sudden rush of additional blood to further deepen the pink in her cheeks and along her neck.

"We blondes never adapt to this kind of heat and humidity as well as you luckier dark-complexioned people do."

He opened the door to the outside, and she stepped through. She was determined, this time around, to insist he keep his hand to himself. If the two got separated in the hustle, it was fate, karma, luck, or whatever else people wanted to call it. So why was she disappointed to find the sidewalk traffic ebbed to a mere trickle, giving Jeff with no excuse to do anything but walk harmlessly along beside her?

"Do we get a water taxi, car taxi, tuk tuk, mini-bus, public bus, or do we walk?"

"Water taxi," she selected. Walking might have been okay on the way to church, but it was no longer a viable alternative. As for taking any of the other means of transportation, the ongoing curb-to-curb traffic jam would mean she'd spend even more time with Jeff than if they walked.

They proceeded southwest on Ratchawong Road and aimed for the Chao Phraya River straight ahead.

"So, tell me more about Jessica Miller," Jeff prodded.

There were just enough people on the sidewalk to keep Jeff's arm periodically rubbing against hers. As it was hardly his fault, she could hardly complain. But it heightened her awareness of him.

"There's really not much more to tell," she parried and wondered why she was clamming up. Up until now, she'd always been eager to promote herself and her designs to anyone, anywhere.

"I should tell you that mystery only makes me more curious," Jeff coaxed.

"I can assure you there are no deep-dark secrets in any of my closets," Jessica insisted. But her denial made it sound just the opposite. Her life had been hard work and more of it. "I merely mean that I already told you all of it on our fateful trip to church this morning."

"No way do I believe, even for a second, that your life was summed up in those few minutes," Jeff disagreed.

"I'm a dress designer who has had a good deal of success, after a good many years of hard work to get it." That she'd had her share of heartbreak and hard knocks along the way, compounded by her father's untimely death and her mother's terminal illness, wasn't now, nor had it ever been, grist for common consumption. "I'm in Bangkok to buy Thai silk that Roman Whyte will, I hope, still be selling me even after you enlisted my unsuspecting aid in pulling your stunt at church this morning."

"You're right, I do know all of that," Jeff agreed. "Now, it's time for the nitty-gritties, like your favorite color, your favorite flower, your favorite movie, your favorite food."

He couldn't know that no one recently had expressed any desire to learn any of those things. Her life had seemed to degenerate into work and more work. "Green, spider mums, *Out of Africa*, pizza," Jessica said.

"Your favorite city, favorite composer, favorite book, favorite author?" Jeff pressed.

"Rome, Beethoven, *West with the Night*, Robert Ludlum," she answered, only because it was easier than trying to explain why she'd rather not. Especially since she wasn't quite sure just why she truly believed that the less he knew about her, and vice versa, the better off she'd be.

"Not Jeff Billings?" he asked in mock horror, and Jessica didn't immediately get the connection. "Your favorite author? Who's this Robert fellow anyway?"

"Robert Ludlum," she laughed, unable not to. "If it's any consolation, I've recently added 'Read a book by Jeff Billings!' to my list of to-do's."

"In that case. . ." They arrived at the corner of Ratchawong and Songwat and caught a glimpse of the Chao Phraya River. He took her hand before she knew he had it and guided her expertly into the sudden surge of pedestrians braving Songwat's traffic to the accompaniment of honking horns and screams from protesting motorists. ". . . I'll forgive you," he concluded once they'd safely reached the other side.

He turned her loose, and for a moment she felt like a canoe adrift on a shifting tide. Her slight dizziness could easily be attributed to the silliness of any blonde who challenged Bangkok sun, heat, and humidity without a hat. Jessica didn't like hats and seldom wore one, so the no-hat theory was certainly preferable to any notion that Jeff was in any way responsible for the weakness in her knees.

A few minutes further the river, wide, lazy, and chocolate brown, made several slow meanders inside the city before it emptied into the Gulf of Siam.

"Now, about that water taxi," Jeff said.

"Water taxi" was a misnomer, at least when compared to those boats of the same name in Venice. In Bangkok, a water taxi was any floatable object that happened to be on the river at the right place and at the right time. Jessica often availed herself of the service, not only because The Oriental Hotel was so easily accessed from its river dock, but because she preferred traveling by water. Even when the rest of the city was wilting in a swelter of heat and humidity, there always seemed to be a touch of life-saving breeze on the river.

Jeff performed the prerequisite ritual of arm-waving, shouting, and sign language to hail boats. Of the three boats that raced toward shore, a small dugout with a low-power outboard that billowed blue-gray exhaust and trailed an oily rainbow-colored slick in the water was easily going to be the winner. The competition gave up and angled back toward mid-river.

"Looks a little small," Jeff observed as it came nearer. "Want to wave it off for something bigger?"

"It's fine," Jessica decided and leaned into the shade of a wooden pile to await its arrival. She saw the boat as the fastest thing available to get her to her hotel. The sooner she got to her hotel, the sooner she would have some time to herself in which to put things in better perspective and decide the ramifications, if any, this morning and noon had had on her life, on her business, and on her happiness.

She watched a Thai captain, stripped to his waist and wearing a pair of pants so spotlessly white that they could blind from a distance, angle his boat for a landing.

"Hello there!" he called, almost maneuvering to where Jeff and Jessica could conveniently board without getting their feet wet. "Americans?"

"Right!" Jeff confirmed, and Jessica, for not the first time in her travels abroad, wondered what it was about Americans that so distinctly set them apart, at a glance, from their German, French, or even British counterparts.

"Great!" the boatman responded, and Jessica saw he was younger than she thought. Or, maybe he was older than he looked, which was more likely in a country where old people could look like teenagers. Whoever found a way to bottle their secret would make a fortune.

Jessica left her savored bit of shade, not in the least worried that the man's enthusiasm portended a con man out to bilk them out of their Yankee dollars. On the whole, she had found Thai people honest and naturally friendly. Granted, there were factions among them, like the dissident Ron Ron group, who were always up to some new mischief. The bombing of the Northwest Orient reservation office at the Siam Center, the last in a recent wave of such terrorist activities, was an excellent case in point. But the U.S. had sent in a member of the Bangkok Branch, Tim Spencer, to take care of that.

"I speak English," the Thai captain boasted, and steadied his boat while Jeff prepared to help Jessica aboard. Jeff's right hand cupped her elbow while his left hand enclosed hers with reassuring confidence.

"And you speak it very well, too," Jessica complimented, enjoying the Thai's responding wide grin that made him look even younger.

"From Chicago?" he asked as Jessica settled into one of the small seats just before a sudden wake from a passing launch caused the smaller boat to rock precariously on the swells. "I have a cousin in Chicago," he boasted proudly.

Suddenly she heard the sharp retort of a car backfiring, and the wooden side of the boat splintered only a few short inches from her left arm. Reflexively, she jerked back and sent the boat into an even more passionate dancing on the waves.

2

The Thai boatman went overboard, and Jeff grabbed her off the seat, sandwiching her between him and the boat bottom. Gasping in surprise, she inhaled a combination of dead fish, fetid water, and Jeff's citrusy cologne. With her face pressed against damp and spongy wood, it took her a minute to understand what had happened. Someone had shot at them! And Jeff had saved her. Or at least gotten her out of harm's way.

His chivalry gave her a warm, tender feeling even in the face of her growing panic.

But she could see where the bullet had blasted through the rotten wood, and a new fear surfaced. Another bullet might penetrate the deteriorating wood and enter warm and yielding flesh. Or it might open the boat to the river. Which would be worse than a quick, merciful death by firing squad. The river was a catchall for sewage and pollutants. Germs and horrible parasites thrived in its waters. Neither Jeff nor Jessica possessed those necessary immunities enjoyed by locals. They needed to get out of there quickly.

"Are you okay?" Jeff asked, his voice breathless, and his heartbeat a timpani, its violent and runaway rataplan coinciding with Jessica's frantically pumping heart.

"My arm," she said.

"Shot?" he asked with obvious concern, his mouth close to her ear, his breath warm against her cheek.

"It's falling asleep."

"Hope it's not the boring company," he said.

She began to laugh, a little hysterically. Breathing deeply to calm herself, she tried to control her fear. At least they weren't dead yet. She wasn't so sure about their boatman.

"Who's shooting?" she asked and wondered if Jeff would tell her if he knew.

"I'd love to know," he replied with the vagueness Jessica somehow expected.

One thing Jessica knew was that *she* didn't recall doing anything lately to make anyone mad enough to come gunning for her.

The boat rocked in another set of waves caused by a larger boat passing on the river. "What if they try again?" That other peoples' lives were proceeding normally around them didn't ease the panic.

"You stay here and keep down." Jeff shifted his weight slowly to his knees.

"Where are you going? You can't leave me here!" She grabbed him.

With a low laugh, he firmly released himself from her hold.

"As much as I wanted to get you alone, this isn't what I had in mind." Once again he impressed her with his ability to keep his humor in a crisis. Slowly he lifted his head above the side of the boat.

"Wait! They may still be there." Knowing that a couple well-aimed shots could still blow them away kept Jessica's heart in her throat, but Jeff's unruffled calm eased some of the fear.

"The coast looks clear," he said. "And we can't stay here all day, can we?"

"You mean we really do have to stop meeting like this?" Jessica asked, pleased that she too could sound calm in the face of full-blown panic.

"That's the way," he encouraged and gave her shoulder a reassuring squeeze.

With no further warning, he was up and gone. The boat bobbed as he left it, and the sun, no longer blocked by his body, exploded its brightness on Jessica's eyes.

She cradled her head on one arm and tried to work the needle-pricks out of the other. She couldn't believe she was here in a coffin-small boat, floating up and down, back and forth, as if in isolation from the rest of the world. Water sloshed against the boat and against the shoreline, but the rotting wood of the boat muted the sound. The loudest thing in Jessica's universe was her galloping heartbeat.

She looked at her wristwatch, but it had stopped, its crystal shattered. It seemed ages since Jeff left, but it might have only been seconds.

She should have been the one who'd gone for help, because she remained convinced no one wanted to kill her. Oh, she hadn't come through life without making a few enemies, no matter how hard she'd genuinely tried not to.

There was Jerry Grear, angry that she'd let him go because of slipshod beadwork. But Jerry, staked out on a Bangkok rooftop, high-powered rifle in hand? Or Henry Smythe-Wilson, who had called her several unkind names when she'd decided to go out on her own instead of letting him continue making all the money off her designs. Suzie Branlic who was mad at Jessica because. . .

Suddenly a hand clutched the edge of the boat, dripping water like blood and tilting the boat sideways. Another hand joined the first, and the boat tipped more precariously. Jessica's heart skipped a beat, then bounced to lodge in her throat. She tried to scream, but nothing came.

A head followed the hands, water-soaked hair plastered like black seaweed over its skull. Jessica's voice returned with a shriek loud enough to wake the dead.

The head and hands disappeared, but she refused to wait for more. Jumping from the boat, she landed in three feet of water, but that didn't stop her forward momentum. She was out of the dirty river faster than even the most athletic parasite could take hold and dig in.

Propelled by fear, she heard only the drumroll of her heart. In her panic, the world was a blur, a terrifying kaleidoscope of color. Unable to focus, she abruptly hit something with the force of a wrecking ball whacking a steel-fortified building. She tried to fight her way past the obstacle. But this was Jeff. He wrapped his arms around her, his soothing voice slowly penetrating her mind's insulating fog.

"It's okay, it's okay," he repeated, and finally she believed him. At least she did until it struck her that it couldn't possibly be okay when she'd been shot at one moment and attacked by the Creature from the Black

Lagoon the next.

She turned back toward the river, her torque so forceful it broke Jeff's hold.

What greeted her wasn't what she expected. Her Monster from the Deep had metamorphosed into the bedraggled and waterlogged Thai boatman, his pants no longer sparkling white but graveyard brown. He stood knee-deep in river water, watching his empty dugout drift downriver.

"We'll need the boat as evidence," someone said, and Jessica realized Jeff had brought a Thai policeman with him. "I'll radio from the car and have someone intercept it."

"Am I pleased to see the police," Jessica said as the officer jogged toward his squad car hidden somewhere within the crowd that had gathered. "Better late than never, I always say."

"Actually, he was on his way when I ran into him," Jeff admitted. "He heard the shot, and a lot of fingers were pointed in our direction."

With Jeff's arms around her, Jessica felt secure for the first time since the gunshot, as if his strength alone protected her. But she also knew that the sense of safety was only an illusion. What, after all, did she really know about him?

"I'm fine," she said and reluctantly pushed free of the cocoon made by Jeff's arms.

"You're sure?" His fingertips lingered on her arm, as if he, too, wanted to maintain the contact.

"Yes, thank-you." She knew she must look horribly disheveled to the gathered crowd. She didn't have a mirror, since her purse had floated away with the boat, but her face was probably filthy from hugging rotting wood. She combed her fingers through her hair, only to meet snarls and tangles. The bottom of her dress was soaked, muddy, and clinging to her legs.

"You look marvelous," Jeff complimented with a glint in his eye. Before Jessica could retort the policeman returned with two associates. The newcomers bypassed Jeff and Jessica for the poor boatman.

The first officer escorted Jessica and Jeff to his squad car and dispersed the rest of the throng. "You will be more comfortable at the station," he told them in good English, then turned the car into the honking Bangkok traffic.

The station was more comfortable than the river bank, and it offered more privacy, but that was all Jessica could say for it.

Jeff and the Thai boatman were ushered down a hall, and Jessica found herself turned over to Police Inspector Chaub. He showed her to the bathroom and placed a guard outside to assure her privacy. The room layout resembled the ladies' rooms she'd encountered while "going native" elsewhere in Bangkok. To her surprise and dismay, she discovered her long-harbored secret suspicions that men enjoyed better than just hole-in-the-floor facilities were wrong. Even the mirror was as cracked and discolored as the one in the women's loo at the Spicy Whiskey. How long ago that seemed!

She used her fingers to restore some semblance of order to her hair. Inspector Chuab had informed her that her purse would be returned as soon as it and the little runaway boat were recovered from the river. Luckily, Jessica had a clean handkerchief in the pocket of her dress which she used to clean off the worst of the grime on her face.

When she rejoined Inspector Chuab, he offered her

tea or coffee, but Jessica never drank either, so the inspector abstained, too. The questions and answers went on from there, and the process was as tiring as Jessica had been led to believe by television crime stories. What it wasn't, as opposed to those same TV shows, was demeaning or in any way violent. From the start, Inspector Chuab made it consolingly clear he suspected the reason behind the attack, and it had nothing whatsoever to do with Jessica. Nevertheless, he routinely made her thoroughly examine her past for anyone who might be out to kill or scare her.

"I suppose you know what they think?" Jeff said when, a few hours later, he followed Jessica into the back of the squad car assigned to take them to their hotel.

"I only know what Inspector Chuab thinks," Jessica responded and sank into a seat she wished were more comfortable. A dull ache pulled at both ends of her spine.

"Inspector Chuab is the old man who hogged you in his office all afternoon?" Jeff asked, slumping down into the seat like a tired dog settling in for the night.

"Inspector Chuab was a perfect gentleman."

"He thinks one of your ex-boyfriends is out to get you, and get me for being your latest one truelove, right?" Jeff laid his head back and shut his eyes. "I agree with him, because I know how killing mad I'd be if I had you, then lost you to another man."

"Actually, he doesn't think it was attempted murder at all." Jessica didn't bother refuting the rest, because she knew Jeff didn't mean it.

"Well, it's possible your old beau just wanted to scare me away," Jeff conceded, "content with me not having you if he can't. That would explain the one bullet when he certainly had time to squeeze off a few more. Without half trying, he could have made Swiss cheese of that rotten boat and of us."

"Inspector Chuab says Powell Whyte had a lot of friends here in Bangkok," Jessica said, and she knew Jeff and she were talking about the same thing, despite his ramblings about a killer boyfriend. "If it hadn't been for Powell hand-carrying examples of Thai silk to potential U.S. and European buyers at the end of World War II, a presently very lucrative industry would have become extinct."

"You don't say?" Jeff didn't sound impressed. He looked tired, and Jessica suddenly suspected his interrogation hadn't been as accommodating as hers.

"Were they pretty rough on you back there?" All sorts of uncomfortable images rose in her mind. Even if Powell Whyte's reputation were as clean as newly driven snow, and Jeff were some scandalmonger out to falsely muddy it from one corner of the world to the other, that was no excuse for someone taking potshots at them.

Jeff opened his eyes, turned his head in her direction, and smiled his usual good cheer. "You mean, did they pull out the thumbscrews, rubber hoses, and the electric cattle prods?" he asked. He leaned forward, as if addressing their chauffeur cum policeman. "Did you use those on me, Jeeves?" When he got no response, he settled back and turned another smile in Jessica's direction. "Naw! They were actually quite civilized. Although they made it clear they disapproved of my being in Bankok doing what I'm doing. Something about Powell Whyte having been quite generous to the people of Thailand. I do recall your knowing he left them the bulk of his extensive collection of Thai artwork, most of which is still in Los Angeles and supposedly scheduled for shipment to Thailand."

"You know the first shipment has already arrived at the museum," she replied.

"Ah, yes, at the museum. One of the very important prerequisites set down by Powell Whyte in his will before Thailand got the valuable prize: 'The people of Thailand must construct and maintain the Powell Whyte Memorial Museum which will house said collection,' " Jeff quoted in a sepuchral monotone. "A museum to be built and operated from a trust fund Whyte laid aside for those purposes, complete with stringent security arrangements to protect the treasures. For if the museum wasn't built, and/or adequate security wasn't provided, the trust is dissolved, its monies *and* the collection reverting to. . ." He locked his gaze with hers. "To guess whom, Jessica?"

"To Roman." She wasn't sure if she'd ever seen all of the detailed text of the will spelled out, but she knew, as did most everyone, that Roman had been Powell Whyte's chief beneficiary.

"Give the lady a Kewpie doll! If the Thais foul up, Roman gets the whole ball of wax." He sounded as if he'd made a very important point, but, if he had, Jessica hadn't followed it. The museum was already built, the first part of the Powell Whyte Collection already installed. A gala celebration was scheduled for the very next weekend, and Jessica's engraved invitation had been hand-delivered to her at the hotel.

Jeff shut his eyes again, and the conversation ebbed. Jessica thought he'd fallen asleep, and she was sorry the intersection of New Road and Si-Phya foretold only a short nap for him before they arrived at their hotel.

"In any of your recent conversations with Roman, has he mentioned any problem at the museum?" Jeff mumbled sleepily. However tired he was, Jessica intuitively sensed something deeper in his question.

"What kind of problem?"

"Oh, I don't know." It sounded to Jessica as if a battle were waging between his talking and his sleeping, and the latter was about to win. "Maybe a crack in the foundation, a rain gutter that doesn't work, or a misplaced figure of a bodhisattva, pre-Ankor style?"

"A misplaced what?"

Her response apparently answered Jeff's question. "Apparently, none of the above," he responded wearily.

"Who said a bodhisattva was misplaced?" Jessica had been at the museum during part of the uncrating of artifacts, and she recalled at least three representations of deities worshiped in Mahayana Buddhism as enlightened ones who'd compassionately refrained from entering nirvana in order to save others. Pre-Ankor style, though, didn't ring any immediate bells.

"Rumors, only rumors," Jeff shrugged off. "One can never place much faith in rumors, only try to check them out. Since Roman absolutely refuses me access to the museum untl it's officially opened, I just thought I'd check with you."

"The museum will be open to the general public in a few days," Jessica reminded. "Check it out then."

"At least the opening is presently *scheduled* for a few days' time," Jeff admitted, and Jessica didn't miss his emphasis.

"You don't believe it'll come off?" She wondered what he was getting at.

"All I believe, at the moment, is that we're about at our hotel." The car correspondingly turned right off New Road onto Oriental Lane. "Which brings me to one final subject. I assume Inspector Chuab suggested you steer clear of me after today. Undoubtedly so that an innocent bystander, like myself, won't, once again, be put at risk by your jealous boyfriend."

"Right," Jessica agreed noncommitally. Inspector Chuab had based his suggestion that she give Jeff a wide berth on his theory that Jeff would remain a target for harassment. After all, the Thai silk industry alone, which Powell Whyte was attributed to have single-handedly brought to its present lucrative position in the world market, employed literally thousands of people. Any one of them might see Jeff's crusade to crucify "the patron saint of Thai silk" as sacrilege. Nor was Whyte Silk Consortium the late Powell Whyte's only link to the country's industries. Which meant that Jessica, or anyone else in Jeff's company, could possibly expect to fall victim to any other stray bullets that might be fired in Jeff's direction. Of course, the Thai police were prepared to do everything in their power to prevent a further incident. However, short of expelling Jeff from the country, they only hoped Jeff would see the light and leave of his own accord.

The car stopped at the street entrance to The Oriental Hotel, and Jeff turned to Jessica. "If Inspector Chuab has spelled it out to you already, it'll save me from going over the reasons as to why it's been very nice to know you, but this has to be good-bye. A pity. I foresaw definite possibilities for the two of us. Unfortunately, we obviously should have met at some other time, in some other place, under far more auspicious stars. Ciao!"

As he left the car, Jessica wondered if she shouldn't ignore Inspector Chuab's warnings. Dropping Jeff on her own was one thing, but being forced into it by some gun-toting fanatic left a bitter taste in her mouth. On the other hand, she didn't want any repeats of that afternoon. Unlike some people who might thrive on such excitement, Jessica had found her overdose of adrenaline almost fatal. She was a dress designer, not some target in an amusement-park arcade.

Still, as she thanked the driver, who still showed no more indication of understanding English, she knew that under different circumstances she would want to pursue whatever it was that drew her to Jeff.

"However, life goes on," Jessica told herself as the police car disappeared down the street, and Jeff disappeared into the hotel.

The doorman in livery tipped his hat, gave her a welcome-to-The-Oriental-Hotel smile and opened the door with a flourish.

Jessica paused, as she invariably did whenever she entered the impressive lobby via the nondescript street entrance. The hotel had been built in the 1870s when the only really convenient transportation was by water and was designed for access and viewing from the Chao Phraya River. No one could appreciate its full grandeur unless they arrived by water. Only then did the pedimented and ornamental facade of the hotel's older building hold its own beside its modern 350-room River Wing. The view from the impressive boat landing accentuated the sweep of green lawns, the jewel of a swimming pool, the old-world veranda, the verdant and multi-fountained gardens, and the two classical lamp-carrying statues. It had all once been owned by the son of Aura Leonoueus, a woman romanticized in *The King and I*, and still it was a magnet for kings, queens, potentates, diplomats, artists, and actors. While here, Somerset Maugham wrote his *The*

Gentleman in the Parlour, and the ghost of Joseph Conrad
was still reported to wander the terraces overlooking the
river.

"And Jeff Billings, infamous author of unauthorized
biographies, is staying here now," Jessica said, and that,
for whatever the inexplicable reason, made her smile.
Maybe because a nearby hotel guest, an Indian gentleman
complete with turban, turned away in obvious embarrassment for the disheveled American who talked to herself.

Jessica picked up her messages at the front desk.
There was no note from Roman. Did that make her
uneasy? No, she didn't think so. Not yet, anyway.

On the way to the elevator, Jessica saw no trace of
Jeff, and she wondered if he had really disappeared so
quickly from her life.

Her room was a welcome sight, and her first order of
business was a bath made possible by the notice in The
Oriental Hotel Directory of Services: "This hotel has its
own sophisticated filtration and purification plant." For
drinking, Jessica still stuck to bottled water.

She sank into the deep lavender-scented bubbles, and
let the dust, dirt, grime, and fatigue of the day soak away
in the decadent luxuriousness of creamy soap and hot
water. Shampooing her hair three times also served to
clean the cobwebs from her brain.

A rigorous rub of a rough and heated Turkish towel
made her feel human again, and she revised all earlier
plans to have supper in her room. Isolated by time and
distance from the horror of the day, and fortified by her
bath, she suddenly didn't want to eat alone. She'd devoted
too much of her life to overcoming a basic cowardice
about entering a restaurant alone. She'd gritted her teeth,
in those early days, and faced down a paranoia that told

her everyone stared at her whenever a waiter disdainfully led her through a crowded dining room of couples to some isolated table off the kitchen. Likewise, she had braved countless wine stewards and their airs of snobbish putdown every time she had said no to a Chateau this or a vintage that. It had been a long haul, but now she could derive a good deal of enjoyment from dining out without a man along. Not that she didn't, on occasion, still opt for room service when she was too tired for anything else. Tonight she felt wonderful, in spite of the events of the day, so she picked up the telephone and made a reservation in the Normandie Room.

She dialed the hotel concierge directly. She always tipped him first thing after checking into the hotel, and last thing as she was checking out. The quantity of the latter depended upon how well he performed such little miracles as getting Jessica into the popular hotel restaurant on such short notice on a busy Sunday night. He'd performed difficult services before, like when he'd arranged for Jessica to get a peek at the dry-docked Royal Barge, *Sri Suphannahongse*, Golden Swan, only seen by the general public on state occasions. Nor did he disappoint this time. Within two minutes, he called back to say a window table was ready whenever she was.

She wore a white puff-sleeve blouse and a long black skirt. Dressing for herself was easier and faster than dressing for a date. While she would never appear in a public place without doing all she could to make herself presentable, she admittedly spent less time than if Jeff, or even Roman, had invited her for supper. There were little tricks of makeup that could dramatically emphasize her eyes, further hollow her cheeks, and highlight her cheek-bones, but she discarded them in favor of a quick application of foundation, powder, lip blush and a dab of perfume behind each ear.

Louis, the Normandie Room maitre d', greeted Jessica by name and showed her to the table George had promised. Her view of the Chao Phraya River through the special floor-to-ceiling, armored, heat-resistant windows always captured Jessica's imagination with a sense of beauty and romanticism and brought her back to this place time and again.

Concentrating on the view, she ordered a duplicate of a meal originally served at the hotel on 20 April 1894: celery soup, fish in red sauce, fried veal with capers, potatoes, green salad, Siamese curry, and baked custard.

Out on the water she spotted the lights of a small dugout and hoped the police had tracked down the other drifting boat with her purse. And the bullet hole, of course. It wasn't much, but it was the only available clue.

"May I join you?" Roman's voice broke her reverie and she turned to him in surprise.

"Of course." Simultaneously the effervescent Louis arrived, wondering if there was anything Monsieur Whyte would like.

"Nothing, thank-you, Louis," Roman declined. "I'm only here for a moment."

Louis was noticeably disappointed, and, frankly, so was Jessica.

"I was going to call you first thing tomorrow," Jessica said as soon as Louis was gone.

"Not trusting me to get around to apologizing before then?" Roman asked.

"Apologize?" Jessica feigned surprise. "Whatever for?"

"For thinking, maybe for even a quick second, that

you and that Billings character were in cahoots," Roman confessed. "For which I *do* apologize."

"Ready to admit Jeff and I were but two innocent ships passing in the night?" Jessica kept to herself an audible sigh of relief. She'd known all along she could count on Roman, but that he'd come through made her life so much easier and more enjoyable.

"Well, I'll admit to one innocent ship," Roman compromised, his blue eyes, far darker than his light-blue shirt, sparkling in the subdued lighting. "You do know he proposes to do a hatchet job on my uncle?"

"I think he calls it a biography," Jessica said, her joking tone keeping the conversation suitably light.

"Yes, and I hear there were people who once called the moon green cheese." Roman arched his left eyebrow, then made a skillful and smooth transition, "I also hear you and he got yourselves shot at this afternoon."

"Which scared me to death." Jessica suppressed a chill. She broke off a piece of hard roll and watched the waiter deliver her soup.

"Inspector Chuab called me about it," Roman said, once the waiter was gone. His gold signet ring caught the light and reflected it.

"I suspected he might." But Jessica wished the inspector hadn't been such a gossip. Roman would certainly wonder why she'd been off with Jeff after the incident on the church steps. "The inspector has only good things to say about the Whyte family, past and present."

"Well, actually, it wasn't so much a courtesy call. He was checking up on a suspect to a crime," Roman said with a wry smile.

"You're joking!"

"It seems as if your friend insinuated to the police that

I might be behind the shooting."

"The man is a certifiable jerk!" Jessica insisted, her new opinion of Jeff in no way tempered by Roman's smile which said he'd survived the slander.

"I suspect he just doesn't know me as well as you do. He and I didn't exactly part as friends, did we?"

"But for him even to have suggested such a thing!" Jessica continued incredulously.

"Luckily, I was at the museum at the time of the shooting, taking care of a little problem," Roman told her. "Enough people saw me there to convince even Mr. Billings that I couldn't have been in two places at once."

"I still can't believe he'd come up with such a hair-brained accusation."

"Anyway." Roman lifted his hand in a dismissing wave. "I was relieved to hear you came through unscathed, although I'm more than a little upset Billings put you in jeopardy."

Because Roman was gentleman enough not to pry for an explanation of why she and Jeff had been together at the boat, Jessica found herself eagerly filling him in. "You know, after you left him at the church, he followed me down the street and promised he was going to go to you and confess how he'd suckered me in."

"Well, if he's sincere in his promise, he's less a scoundrel than I thought," Roman conceded. "Of course, you'll excuse me if I withhold final judgment until I see if he follows through. Words are a dime a dozen, and so far there's been no sign of his knocking on my door."

"In all truth, I told him not to bother," Jessica confessed. "I said you and I went back far enough that you didn't need his two-cents' worth."

"Bravo! Besides, he probably planned to use it as

another way of getting to me. Muckrakers will go to any lengths when they think, deluded or not, that they're hot on a story."

"Have you ever read anything he's written?" Jessica knew her seemingly innocent question could easily be misinterpreted as criticism of how Roman and she weren't giving Jeff a fair shake without having personally examined his past efforts.

"Actually, I'm in the middle of his six-hundred pages on Terrence McAter," Roman said, surprising her. Then again, she should have remembered Roman's reputation for being fair. As it was, she felt disloyal for having wondered if Roman's dislike of Jeff were based more upon a fear of Jeff proving certain rumors true, rather than on any real proof of Jeff's lack of writing scruples. "I'll lend it to you when I'm finished," Roman offered. "I'll even admit it's not nearly as trashy an expose as I expected. On the other hand, I think Billings would be a little out of his depth in writing about someone not ear-deep in nefarious munitions deals or clandestine political machinations."

"You mean a subject like your uncle?" Jessica had heard the whispered innuendos about Powell Whyte, and she was sure Roman must have heard them too, long before Jeff entered the picture. If the rumors were true, weren't they best kept sequestered in the closet? "Don't you think that your uncle has done so much for Thailand that his story deserves to be told?" she wondered aloud. Roman's expression changed, making her feel guilty, as if she'd chosen Jeff instead of him for her after-school soccer team. She wanted to erase that look from his handsome face. She did think it important, however, that he be realistic. If there were fire where Jeff had spotted smoke, someone would eventually expose the facts, even if Jeff didn't.

She took a deep breath and plowed ahead, desperate for the words to put across what was really important here: "There was a horse thief in my family," she said, and he grimaced noticeably at the comparison. "My father used to tell me how every time someone mentioned that John Miller had thieved horses and had been hanged for his efforts, my Dad's grandmother would go to her room and lock herself in." Jessica hurried on, because there was a point to be made here. "Whenever I heard that story, I wondered why Great-grandma should have been embarrassed. She hadn't been responsible for what he did. She couldn't be blamed for what happened to him."

"Well, wouldn't it be nice if we were always judged on our own merits?" Roman said, and somehow didn't sound patronizing.

"Since we're both Americans, we know of a well-respected President who wouldn't have gotten where he was if he'd let himself be encumbered by the rumors that linked his father to bootleg whiskey during Prohibition, don't we?" Jessica continued. "I say if he could be his own man, anyone can."

Roman looked as if he were going to say something, but the arrival of the waiter who wanted to know if there was anything wrong with Jessica's untouched soup stopped him. The concoction of celery sat, obviously the worse for its neglect.

"Why don't you bring her another bowl?" Roman suggested. "I'm afraid I've kept her helplessly distracted with my small talk."

"Of course, Mr. Whyte." The waiter proceeded to remove the cool bowl.

"What was the problem at the museum?" Jessica

asked, because she suddenly wanted to change the subject. She'd said all she wanted about Jeff Billings and Powell Whyte. She'd probably said too much, and it might have seemed she was pleading Jeff's case, when she hadn't meant to do any such thing.

"Who said there was a problem at the museum?" he asked, making it seem as if Jessica had just accused the President of the U.S. of selling arms to Libya.

"*You* did. Inspector Chuab called to see if you were shooting a rifle at Jeff and me, and you said you were at the museum, 'taking care of a little problem.' " She couldn't admit that Jeff had clued her in to the possibility of a problem. She didn't want to go back to where that would take them.

"Hopefully, you won't mention that to anyone else." Roman made it seem as if this were some kind of secret regarding world security.

"How can I mention details I don't have?" Jessica said, hinting that he should feel free to tell her more.

Apparently not willing to volunteer any real insight, he shifted their conversation. "How would you like a bit of good news?"

Jessica couldn't switch subjects in her mind so easily and she almost asked outright if it were true one of the newly arrived bodhisattvas had been misplaced. But she caught herself in time. He'd want to know where she'd heard that, and off they'd go again. She wished Jeff had never intruded himself into her life.

"I can always use good news," she said, and, as if on cue, the waiter arrived with her fresh bowl of hot celery soup. She sampled the essence of a green vegetable and discovered it wasn't nearly as tasty as her earlier *gaeng chud* with Jeff.

"Well, I think you'll agree this news *is* good," Roman prophesied. "However, since it is business-related, and. . ."

Jessica waited, her curiosity piqued, confused that he didn't just fill in the blank. Then she smiled in quick understanding. "Oh, I see!"

". . . today is Sunday," they finished in two-part harmony with accompanying grins.

"So, if you promise to save tomorrow for me, I'll leave you before your soup gets cold a second time."

"I promise, but I'd like to know what kind of friend says things he knows will keep me awake all night pondering the possibilities?"

"We'll make a day of it." Roman pushed back his chair in order to get to his feet. "Why don't I pick you up in the morning at eight sharp? We'll take a business trip up north and have a picnic to boot."

"Up north? I'm getting curiouser and curiouser."

"Tomorrow it is!" He came around the table to deliver a perfunctory kiss to her forehead.

Jessica momentarily waxed nostalgic for that year of their lives when it was red roses and spider mums; moonlight and toasty sunshine; laughter and tears. But her reflection on the past dissipated quickly. If all of the right magic had been there, they would have found it. They'd certainly looked hard enough, unwilling to surrender their dream easily. But they *had* surrendered it. They'd moved on, and Jessica knew she didn't want to go back — not really. Her friendship with Roman had become an important part of her life which worked far better for both of them than marriage would have. They were two people, both looking for mates with whom to share a love for all eternity, and neither of them had been prepared to accept second best.

She put a hand on his forearm and gave it a squeeze, and memories of what she felt when she touched Jeff blew into her mind. Quickly, she suppressed them. The last thing she needed was to complicate her life with thoughts of Jeff.

"I did tell you how glad I was you came out of your little experience safely?" he asked, his hand on hers, his grip friendly, reassuring, even affectionate; not electric — never electric.

"Yes," she said. "Thanks for caring."

He left behind him a complex fragrance of expensive cologne: vanilla, sandalwood, and musk, all mixed in with other exotic aromas Jessica couldn't classify. Jeff, on the other hand, smelled of lemon, pure, unadulterated, and pleasingly simple.

With Jeff once again intruding himself on her mind, she absently returned to her soup, then decided she'd had enough of it and Jeff. She laid her spoon on the edge of the supporting plate to signal she was finished. The waiter, right on cue, spirited the soup away and returned shortly with fish delectably moist and flaky in red sauce. It took Jessica less than two bites to know she wasn't in the mood to give even these subtle flavors their justice. She blamed it all on Jeff and the day. Where was Jeff, and what was he doing? Was he lined up in the cross hairs of yet another rifle sight?

"Mademoiselle Miller?"

Jessica jumped at Louis's unexpected interruption of her macabre reverie, embarrassed that she hadn't noticed his approach.

"You've a phone call," he said without producing the phone for the convenient plug-in in the nearby wall. Evidently he noticed her hesitation. "I'm afraid he's calling in on the pay phone in the foyer."

"Did he give a name?" she asked, unable to imagine anyone so eccentric as to place an inconvenient call that didn't go through the hotel switchboard.

"No, mademoiselle, he didn't."

"Thank you." Laying her napkin to one side, she gave her fish a forgiving look, knowing it would be cold by the time she returned.

She got up, turned toward the foyer, and immediately spotted Tim Spencer among the diners.

Tim was hard to miss because at six-foot-five he could dominate most any room, even when sitting down. The elegant decor of his surroundings only made his masculine physique seem to beg for a more appropriate setting, like a calisthenics field or a sporting arena.

Jessica thought Tim was a very attractive man, which just went to show that a woman didn't have to be a beauty queen to win the marital sweepstakes, because Jessica doubted his wife Nora had ever been truly beautiful. Comparatively plain, Nora was short and tending toward plumpness, but Nora and Tim made a couple that magically complimented each other.

But today Nora wasn't with Tim. As was usually the case whenever Jessica spotted Tim out on the town without his wife, he was with one of his government associates.

His companion was well over six-foot-two and, if obviously younger, didn't automatically win out in any comparisons.

There was something about their short-cropped hair, Tim's white, the other man's blond, and their ramrod postures at the table, that proclaimed military backgrounds.

Jessica decided not to say hello. Not because she

didn't like Tim. He and Nora always went out of their way to make her feel welcome at church or in their home. At least once during each of Jessica's recent trips to Bangkok Nora would call for lunch, delighted when Jessica could accept and blessedly non-temperamental whenever Jessica had to beg off.

But Jessica never knew when Tim might be incognito. Once, when lunching with Nora, they'd stopped at the Jan Chem See Restaurant, where Nora promised Jessica "the very best chicken in the world." Jessica had been readily agreeing that Nora's boasts about the food were all true, when Tim entered the room. "I didn't know Tim was joining us," Jessica had said. Without turning to verify her husband's presence, Nora had said, "He's probably here on business, so we better not acknowledge him unless he comes over." He didn't come over. For all the attention he paid them, they might have been two strangers.

The other time something similar had happened, Jessica had been with Roman at the Nana, eating oven-baked rice in pineapple and busily shelling charcoal-grilled shrimp in a basket. As if by mutual consent neither Jessica nor Roman commented upon Tim's arrival.

So now, in the Normandie Room, Tim surprised her by catching her eye, and breaking in to a wide grin of recognition. "Jessica," he called. "How are you?" He and his companion stood in military unison, making Jessica feel very much a Mutt with two Jeffs. "Nora said you were back, and she wanted to call you for lunch. Clarence," he turned to the other man, "this is Jessica Miller, a designer whose dresses you'll want your wife to steer clear of if you plan to have any money left over for your retirement. Jessica, this is Clarence West, the latest addition to our embassy staff."

"Clarence," Jessica echoed, returning his pleasant smile.

"Nice to meet you." Clarence, like Tim, looked as if he'd be more comfortable in a uniform. His maroon sports jacket, obviously bought off-the-rack, was too tight across his broad shoulders. Jessica expected seams to rip as he took her hand in his massive fingers and gave a firm yet surprisingly gentle shake.

"Are you alone?" Tim, like the diplomat he was, made it sound as if he couldn't believe anyone so charming could be on the loose. However, when a glance in the direction from which she'd come apparently told him she was alone, he insisted, "Join us! Nora is always having you to lunch by herself, and it's about time she got her latest report on your successes from me. You know, she priced one of your little dinner dresses in some fashion magazine sent over by our daughter living in Boston, and she almost expired on our living-room rug."

His laughter was infectious and triggered a show of Clarence's startlingly white teeth and deep dimple. Jessica's responding wide smile was mirrored on the faces of at least five eavesdropping people at nearby tables.

"Unfortunately, I have fish growing cold at my table and a telephone call awaiting me in the foyer," Jessica apologized.

"A call in the foyer?" Tim asked, and it was obvious he found that as strange as Jessica did.

"It's on the pay phone," Jessica explained.

"Sounds as if I'm not the only one with inconsiderate friends," Tim said. "If I were you, I'd have Louis tell whomever it is to call you back on the restaurant line. This food is too expensive to abandon for even a few minutes."

"Amen!" Clarence chimed in.

Jessica considered Tim's suggestion, but reluctantly decided against it. "It'll only take me a minute, and then maybe I can join you for dessert." She figured Tim with his ready good humor would be a welcome change from the first part of her day, especially if he hadn't yet heard how she'd gone from church to shooting gallery in one Sunday afternoon. The normalcy of innocent small talk might help her put the abnormal happenings of her exceptional day into better perspective.

She excused herself to find the pay phone. "Hello?"

"Jessica Miller?" a disembodied male voice demanded.

"Who is this, please?"

"Jessica Miller?" the voice persisted. Unsuccessfully, she tried to identify the speaker. What had led her to expect it would be Jeff on the other end?

"Yes, this is Jessica Miller." She felt like asking him whether he thought anyone else would be dumb enough to be out in the foyer, letting her supper go cold.

"I have a certain something that Mr. Billings is anxious to have," the man said. Sure she misheard, she asked him to repeat it, and he did.

"Shouldn't you be speaking with Mr. Billings, then? I'm afraid this has nothing to do with me."

"I've already discussed it with him," the man admitted, and that made even less sense to Jessica.

"I don't see, Mr. . ." she paused with hopes he'd fill in the blank.

"I suggested he let you accompany him to pick up," the man said, "but he refused. I thought you might reconsider, since the package is something Mr. Billings is most anxious to have, and one which I'm most anxious to be rid of."

"I'm not following you, Mr. . . ." She tried again.

"It's not that I don't trust Mr. Billings any less than I would anyone under these same circumstances," he said, and Jessica decided it was hopeless to continue her efforts to get him to identify himself. "I'm merely cautious. He should be less inclined to try anything funny if he has you along to worry about."

"Is this some kind of joke?"

"No joke, Miss Miller. Quite to the contrary, I'm deadly serious."

"Then, I really must insist that this is between you and Mr. Billings," Jessica said with finality. "This has nothing whatsoever to do with me."

"Mr. Billings was obviously concerned for your safety during a rather unfortunate incident on the bank of the Chao Phraya this afternoon."

"*You* fired that rifle!" Jessica said so loudly that Louis, at his desk, looked up and frowned.

"No, not I," the voice denied. "Nor did the man I had watching Mr. Billings at the time."

"You were having Jeff followed?" The idea appalled her. It was too fantastic. But then, wasn't all of it?

"I think Mr. Billings better put things into perspective for you. Why don't you make it a point to ask him about it, and I'll call you back, same time, same place, tomorrow night?"

"I'm going to be out all day tomorrow." If he thought she was going to let any Jeff-related matter interfere with her picnic with Roman, and her business surprise, he was sadly mistaken. "I haven't the faintest idea what time I'll be back."

"Most unfortunate," the man replied and sounded genuinely upset.

With a click, the phone went dead.

"Hello! Hello"

Louis looked up again, and Jessica replaced the receiver with a minimum of noise. What was that call all about? Nothing the man said made sense. What did he have for Jeff that required Jessica along for the ride? Why did he think she could influence Jeff or would want to? The whole thing was patently absurd, one more complication in her life — courtesy of Jeff Billings. Besides, her fish in red sauce was getting cold, and Tim and Clarence were waiting.

She took three steps toward the dining area, and everything exploded in a sudden flash of blinding heat and light. With the subtlety of a freight train, a giant force picked her up and bodily slammed her back against the pay phone.

3

While Jessica didn't know where she was, she did know she'd expended a good deal of energy to get there. She was very, very tired, and her entire body ached.

Darkness surrounded her. Not a pinprick of light held the hope of a distant mouth of a well for someone at the very bottom, or a faraway tunnel entrance for someone lost in a mine.

She groaned her exhaustion and her frustration futilely, trying to make sense of what had happened.

"Sleeping beauty is supposed to wait for a kiss from Prince Charming, isn't she?" The asking voice was familiar, but Jessica couldn't place it. She thought it might be Jeff, or Roman, or Inspector Chuab, or Tim Spencer .... No, not Tim, although she didn't exactly know why. Not Clarence West, either.

Jessica felt as if she were in some mad-hatter's dream

She pinched herself, which only let greater aches and pains loose inside her.

Slowly, she realize her eyes were shut. Battling lids that resisted as if heavily weighed down with coagulating glue, she tried to open them. The sudden introduction of light rapidly constricted her pupils, interfering with her efforts to focus in the revealed brightness.

"Where am I?" Bed sheets seemed to materialize as drapery hanging from the ceiling.

"You're safe and sound at the hospital, and the doctor says there probably won't be any lingering after-effects. Short-term ones of course: dizziness, aches, pains, that sort of thing. But, on the whole, you're a very lucky lady."

The reassuring voice became a fuzzy blob that grew increasingly more defined around the edges. "Jeff?" Jessica asked tentatively.

"Right on the money, sweetheart!" Jeff said. "You obviously survived your collision with that wall."

"I don't feel very well." Jessica still couldn't make sense of any of it. She tried to move to a sitting position and actually succeeded with a little help. Only then did she realize she was in a bed and the hanging bed sheets were partitioning curtains.

"I was talking to that man on the phone," she said, then wondered if that were true. She'd finished her conversations with him, hadn't she? "I'm confused," she admitted.

"To be expected," Jeff consoled.

Images of cold soup, cold fish, a view of the Chao Phraya River, Tim Spencer, and a pay telephone, floated in her mind without rhyme or reason.

"The Ron Ron took credit for planting the bomb," Jeff said, soothing her hair off her forehead. His fingers were cool and surprisingly gentle. "The blast was hardly over before a Ron Ron spokesman called the newspapers to proclaim another victory against U.S. imperialist meddling. I'd say this definitely wasn't your lucky day, but you seem to have survived it."

"The Ron Ron?" Jessica vaguely recalled it had claimed responsibility for the bombing of the Northwest Orient reservation office at the Siam Center. Was that the blast to which Jeff referred?

". . . Spencer," Jeff was saying. Jessica missed the first but what she heard filled her with anguish.

"Not Tim?!" There was something frightening in her mind's eye, just on the brink of focusing. Something was very wrong here.

She shouldn't be in a hospital or in bed. She should be at the Normandie Room, eating cold soup and cold fish.

"Were you at the restaurant?" she asked Jeff, because she couldn't remember him being there, although she did recall talking about him with someone.

"Me? I was in my room when the explosion went off and floured me with ceiling plaster."

Jeff's hand again smoothed her forehead, and she captured his fingers in her hands. She gave a reflective squeeze, as if to assure herself this wasn't a dream.

"I knew Tim Spencer from church," Jessica said, not releasing Jeff's hand but kneading it like a cat sharpening its claws on couch upholstery.

"I'm sorry." Jeff added his free hand to the other in Jessica's firm clasp. "Spencer apparently had something to do with U.S. Intelligence, right? He and another fellow. . ."

"Clarence," Jessica identified. "Clarence West."

". . . were both in the restaurant."

"Yes," Jessica acknowledged. She'd stopped by their table. They'd asked her to join them. She'd said yes after. . .. After what?

"I had a call on the pay phone in the foyer," she remembered. That's how she'd excused herself when Tim had asked her to join them: a phone call in the foyer and cold fish on her table. Had she almost asked Louis to have the caller phone back on the restaurant line?

"Well, be sure to thank whomever called you out in time," Jeff insisted. "He got you out of the restaurant alive."

"I didn't know him," she said and raised her hands and Jeff's to her forehead. "I didn't know him," she repeated and shut her eyes.

Her mind replayed it in slow motion: the flash of blinding light, the flying matter, Louis lifted from his disintegrating chair, the starburst of shattering wood, glass, and plastic. She shuddered.

"You're going to be all right, Jessica," Jeff assured. "I promise there are no broken bones, and your disorientation will fade."

"It was horrible!" But the word hardly described it. "Horrible, horrible!"

"I was there a few minutes after it happened," Jeff told her. "I came up the stairs. You were the first person I saw, and . . . ." He moved to sit on the edge of her bed. Wrapping an arm around her, he gave a reassuring hug. She laid her head against his shoulder. She smelled his lemon cologne and that comforted her; he comforted her.

She cried, and she was glad she was crying, because she knew tears were a catharsis. They helped when her father died. They helped when her mother died. They helped now.

"You know, Roman is going to be furious that you regained consciousness on my time," Jeff said cryptically as he reached for several tissues from an open box on a stand by the bed and handed them to her. She wiped her nose and eyes, convinced the world would be a lot better off if men cried, too.

"What about Roman?" she asked and handed Jeff her tear-sopped tissues in exchange for fresh ones.

"He arrived here shortly after your ambulance and would have taken over completely if I hadn't refused to be dislodged. He'd still be in here now, but he's off to find a doctor to tell him why you were still comatose. Rather possessive for just a friend, isn't he?"

"Actually, he's more than a friend," Jessica admitted.

"Ah!" Jeff exclaimed, convincing Jessica she'd misled him. "So, that's it, is it?"

Knowing it might be better to leave him with his misconception, she proceeded to correct it: "More than a friend, but less than what you're making of it."

"Oh?" he asked with amused undertones. "And what am I making of it? No, you needn't answer that, because I suspected something between you two when Roman didn't need my explanations about how you were involved in my sudden appearance at church. Blind trust is a rarity these days."

"We thought about marriage once but settled on friendship," Jessica said. The explosion must have scrambled her brains. Here she was, spilling her private life to a man she'd known for a grand total of . . . . She looked at her wrist for her watch, but it wasn't there. She remembered taking it off in her room at the hotel, the crystal cracked and the mechanism broken. "What time is it?"

He looked at his wristwatch. "About two o'clock Monday morning." Which meant Jessica had known him for less than twenty-four hours. "And, I'm late for an appointment," he added with a frown. "On the other hand . . ." He moved away from Jessica and the bed. Immediately she missed the feel and smell of him. She missed the reassuring warmth and hardness of his body. ". . . I can now head off, knowing you're well on your way to recovery."

"You have an appointment at this time of the morning?" Jessica tried to tell herself that the edge in her voice had nothing whatsoever to do with her disappointment over his deserting her for someone or something else.

"Weird hours come with the territory," Jeff admitted. "In my business, I'm forced to follow other people's time-tables rather than my own. Even you got yourself carted off to the hospital after I'd hit the sack for a few hours of shut-eye."

"You're going to meet that man." Jessica slid farther up in bed and conjured new aches and pains in new places.

"*A* man, certainly," Jeff admitted. "But *that* man?" he queried with a quizzical arch of an eyebrow.

"The man on the phone."

"The man on the phone?" he echoed but made it a question.

"When the bomb went off," Jessica said. "Actually, he'd just rung off before the bomb went. I'd hung up and was heading back." The nightmare gripped her again. Back to eventually join Tim and Clarence for dessert.

Poor Nora! How was she taking it? How would any wife take such news of personal violence? And, what of Clarence's wife? He did have one: Tim had warned him to keep her away from Jessica's dresses if he wanted money for retirement. It seemed inconceivable that they could be dead. What a rotten world when two such men could die over supper!

"Go on," Jeff said to refocus her thoughts.

"He said he had something you wanted, and he wanted to get rid of. He seemed to think I should tag along with you to pick it up."

"And what did you say to his obviously bizarre proposal?"

Unsuccessfully Jessica tried to read Jeff's expression. "I told him I hardly saw where his business with you had anything to do with me."

"And that's exactly what you should have told him, and what you'll tell him again if he's ever stupid enough to call you back!"

"He said you'd discussed the possibility of my coming along," Jessica said, because she wanted to keep him with her. Not only did she enjoy his company, but she didn't want him hurt. If innocent people could get shot at while boarding a water taxi and blown up over supper, she shuddered at what could happen to Jeff on a dark Bangkok street at two o'clock in the morning.

"It was hardly a discussion," Jeff said with a nonchalance in his voice she didn't believe. "He brought up the ludicrous idea, and I told him what he could do with it. It should have stopped there."

"Obviously, it didn't." Jessica paused thoughtfully. "And lucky for me, too. It saved my life."

"Look, I promise the bozo won't bother you again." Jessica saw how his concern continued to center on her.

She decided not to be subtle. "Did it ever occur to you that I might be concerned for your safety?"

"My safety?" he asked with such a startled you've-got-to-be-kidding look that she couldn't help laughing. But the jarring of her bruised insides conjured a quick return to sobriety. "You okay?"

His cool hand came back to her forehead, and Jessica wished he'd keep it there instead of rushing off into the Bangkok night. The man on the phone hadn't sounded like anyone she'd want to meet in broad daylight, let alone at two o'clock in the morning.

"I'm fine," she insisted, then amended, "or, I'm hopefully going to be fine if that doctor you told me about is right. It's just that I've grown somewhat fond of you over the last. . ." She looked at her wrist in pantomime of checking a watch. ". . . eighteen-plus hours."

"I appreciate it," he said and kissed her spontaneously on the forehead. The kiss was as brief as the brush of Roman's lips to the same spot at the restaurant the night before, but with a difference that Jessica didn't want to analyze, as if too close a scrutiny would reveal the mundane. "And your concern," Jeff added with a warm smile that would melt ice. "Very few people have expressed any genuine concern for my well-being since my parents died."

"They're both dead?" Jessica asked, strangely desperate for any personal information he was willing to give her.

"I used to do a good deal of reading as a child," he told her. "Every time I read about a character's parents killed in an auto accident, I'd say: 'Come on, give your readers a break.' As it turned out, though, that happens to a good many people every year. My parents included."

"I'm sorry." In order to make him see how her empathy was legitimate, she added, "My parents are both gone, too. Heart attack. Cancer."

"Were they married in one of your church temples?" When he saw her surprise, he gently chided, "I do know a little something about religion, you know. Or, did you have me down in your book as a confirmed atheist?"

"An atheist?" No, she'd never thought that of him. The unacceptable something she already felt toward him would be even more unacceptable if he didn't believe in God. Religion was so much a part of Jessica's life, she'd never assumed it wasn't part of Jeff's life, too. "I never thought you were an atheist."

"Good, because I am a religious man, in my own way. And I've found a good deal that's worthwhile in the Mormon church. Like your belief in marriage for time and eternity."

"Yes, I'm glad my parents had that." Jessica realized that was the answer to his original question.

He checked his wristwatch, and Jessica knew, with a sudden speeding of her heartbeat, that she'd held him for as long as she could. When she couldn't think of anything more to keep him safely with her, she consoled herself with a promise to pray for his safety after he'd gone.

"One more thing," he said and stepped over to take hold of one curtain and send it scooting on its runners.

"Ohhhhhh!" Jessica exclaimed over the large and small arrangements of spider mums revealed along the far wall.

"This one is from me," Jeff said and pinpointed a modest bouquet in a clear crystal vase. "I only mention that fact because my contribution would have been a bit more impressive if someone we both know hadn't woke up every florist in Bangkok and commandeered every spider mum in the city. You should have heard me ranting, raving, and begging to wrest even these few paltry blooms from a sleepy florist before Roman Whyte could get to him."

"They're beautiful." For some reason, maybe because he'd singled them out, the flowers from him did look more radiant, their greens and whites more dazzling than the rest.

Then, for a moment of seeming miracle, Jeff looked poised on the brink of staying, after all. But the sudden opening of the door evidently decided him the other way. "I'll stop by later to see how you are," he promised, and, with a nod, neither friendly nor hostile to Roman, Jeff disappeared into the hallway.

Roman's glance momentarily followed Jeff's exit but quickly returned to Jessica. "Thank heaven, you're conscious!" he said, coming over to the bed. "How do you feel?"

"A little woozy." She suspected she'd feel better if Jeff hadn't gone off for his early-morning meeting. On the other hand, she argued, who was she to worry about Jeff? He was probably used to nocturnal meetings with sleazy characters. Jessica's needs would be better served by telescoping everything back on herself.

"You look a little warm," Roman said and laid his hand on her forehead. Without really meaning to, Jessica compared his touch with Jeff's. As with their respective kisses-to-her-forehead, there was a difference here, too. "You feel cool, though," Roman concluded, pulling his hand away.

"How's Nora taking Tim's death?" Jessica asked, determined to keep her worries about Jeff in check and to get her thoughts back in perspective. Nora was her friend; Jeff was a mere acquaintance. Therefore, Nora took precedence.

"Jeff told you about Tim, then." Roman's frown indicated he wasn't pleased by Jeff's candidness in the face of Jessica's obviously shaky condition. "Nora's always lived with the possibility that something like this could happen, but that hasn't made the reality any easier. Sister Sycamore and a couple other members of the Branch are with her now."

"Jeff said the Ron Ron group claims responsibility."

"He has been a veritable news service, hasn't he?" Roman frowned. "I would have thought he'd wait for you to get your legs back under you before filling in with all the gory details."

"I'm sure he was only trying to be helpful. I came to with my brains a bit scrambled, and he gave me some points of reference to get me oriented."

"I wonder where he's off to now in such a hurry? Earlier, he gave me the distinct impression he'd moved in here for the duration and a charge of TNT wouldn't dislodge him."

"He said he had a previous appointment he couldn't cancel." Jessica hoped she didn't sound petulant.

"An appointment at two o'clock in the morning?" Roman echoed Jessica's sentiments exactly.

"Someone else's idea, not his," she explained and was tempted to enlist Roman's aid to make sure Jeff wasn't off doing anything foolish. Only her conviction that she had no business involving herself in Jeff's business stopped her. She also suspected Jeff wouldn't appreciate her telling Roman about a meeting that probably concerned Jeff's research on Roman's uncle.

"I suppose he didn't tell you he emerged as somewhat of a hero from all of this." Roman pulled a nearby chair up closer to her bed.

"Jeff, a hero?"

"His room was a couple of floors below the restaurant, and he was quick enough with his wits to be one of the first up the stairs," Roman said. "His quick thinking and skill with a tourniquet actually saved Louis's life if not the poor man's leg."

"Louis? The maitre d'?" Jessica had forgotten all about him. "No, Jeff didn't tell me a word." Then again, she didn't see Jeff as someone who'd toot his own horn. Jeff would have done what was required and thought it in no way extraordinary, the way he'd quickly and automatically inserted himself between Jessica and the sniper. He was all well-honed reflexes and possibly figured he would be doing what any other man would have done under similar circumstances.

"I could almost like the man if. . . ." Roman said and left it hanging.

"If he weren't here to do an unauthorized biography on your uncle, you mean?" Jessica added, finding his partial admission extraordinary.

"Oh, *that* to be sure," Roman said. He turned his full attention on Jessica, locking her gray eyes with his black-streaked blue ones. "I have this sneaking suspicion that he's about to make a 'move' on you, if he hasn't already."

"A move?" Jessica asked incredulously. "For heaven's sake be serious! The man already used me once, remember? Please, do give us both credit for being smarter the second time around."

"Oh, but he didn't purposely use you, don't *you* forget," Roman argued. He marched up to me right here at the hospital and made a clean breast of it. Which was less surprising than his not following up with yet another request for a preview of the Powell Whyte Art Collection.

Something else he said, too: he envied you and me our relationship, because good friends were hard to find in this day
and age. You'll notice, Jessica. . ." He paused as if wanting
to be sure he had her undivided attention. ". . . he made it a
point to call us *friends*. I got the distinct impression he was
waiting for me to argue the point."

"Argue it for what purpose?" Jessica wondered if
Roman could be serious.

"You think maybe he was fishing? The way a man
attracted to a woman might angle to get a better lay of the
land by defining his potential competition?"

"I can't believe you actually said that!" Jessica
wondered how she would take the news if it were true.
Since it wasn't, there was no point in fanciful conjecture.
Meanwhile, she couldn't deny Jeff possessed a certain
something that any woman would find appealing.

"You're denying the sparks, then?" Roman asked.
"When I opened that door a few minutes ago, I could have
sworn there was enough electricity bouncing off these walls
to cause spontaneous combustion."

He settled back in the chair and folded his arms across
his chest. "I see Billings as someone out to cause me big
problems, in more ways than one, in spite of how much I
admire his heroic performance at the hotel."

Alerted by a new note in his voice, Jessica probed
further. "I think you like him."

"Don't misconstrue 'like' for, 'The two of you have my
blessing!' " Roman warned. "I'm not at all sure he'd be the
man for you, even if he converted to Mormonism and a
host of angels came down to sing 'Hallelujah!' in confirmation of his new-found faith." He flashed her a thoroughly
charming grin, the grin that had attracted her to him in the
first place. "Do you think that comes off making me sound

too jealous?"

Jessica laughed. She simply couldn't help it. It was something her psyche demanded to counteract the horror of the nightmare that had put her in the hospital in the first place. It was something that Roman evidently knew she needed.

"This is a comatose patient?" someone asked from the door.

The question from the small-boned Thai doctor, whose thick glasses made his eyes seem larger, only served to increase their laughter. If Jessica could recognize an edge of hysteria in her sounds, she couldn't deny how none of her aches and pains any longer wielded the power to hurt her. For the moment, she was free of all her agony and discomfort.

"Laughter is good medicine," the doctor prescribed.

Managing to regain a measure of control, Roman introduced the doctor. "Jessica Miller, may I present my friend, Dr. Philip Changmai?"

"Doctor," Jessica echoed, feeling wonderfully better and knowing the laughter was responsible.

Dr. Changmai produced a small flashlight and proceeded to examine Jessica's eyes and her reaction to light. He asked her to stretch out her arms and alternately touch her forefingers to her nose.

"Rest, I think," he decided when he was finished. "With doses of laughter to recommence sometime tomorrow, or, rather. . ." He glanced at his watch. ". . . sometime later today."

"She is going to be all right?" Roman asked, as if something bad might have escaped him.

"Everything does point toward that happy prognosis," Dr. Changmai confirmed. He had a pleasant sing-song way of pronouncing his English. "However, we shall monitor her carefully for the next few days, yes?"

"Next few days!" Jessica had an aversion to hospitals, especially after watching her mother die in one.

"A good sign: not looking forward to staying in bed and feasting on hospital victuals," Dr. Changmai said. "On which note, I'll send in a nurse to give the patient a little something to help her sleep."

"I'm going to catch some shut-eye on the next bed, Philip," Roman said.

"That's your perogative, of course," Dr. Changmai consented, "although your own bed would certainly be more comfortable, and Miss Miller isn't going to be up to much small talk after sedation."

"I'll stay," Roman insisted, dismissing all Dr. Changmai's arguments.

"I'll inform the nurses's station that the bed is occupied," Dr. Changmai said with a polite nod before leaving the room.

After the doctor had left, Jessica thanked Roman for the lovely flowers.

Roman glanced in the direction of the blossoms in question. "I suppose you know one group of those, I haven't the faintest idea which, comes to you courtesy of Billings?"

"I think he mentioned something to that effect."

"Nothing could have convinced me more that Billings is a force to be reckoned with than his being able to finagle those mums out of Mr. Sing," Roman said in begrudging compliment. "How do you suppose, Jessica. . ." He paused significantly, ". . . that he happened to know your favorite flower on such short notice?"

"Maybe because he asked me what it was yesterday

afternoon."

"Didn't I tell you the man is F-A-S-T?" Roman shook his head thoughtfully. "Do you recall how long it took me to figure out your preference for spider mums? About six-dozen red roses later."

Before she could answer, the nurse arrived with a daunting needle and syringe.

Miss Chou, or so said her name tag, no-nonsensically ordered Roman to stand beyond the curtain until she administered Jessica's shot to the hip. Once finished, she left, and Roman returned from temporary exile. He took Jessica's hand, and he stood closely by while she grew drowsy.

"No need for you ever to be jealous," she told him. Already the sedative was making her words slow and thick. "I'll always love you as a friend, Roman. Always, always. Always."

"You just get some sleep." His voice soothed her, and his hand squeezed hers in comforting reassurance. "Sleep is just what the doctor ordered."

Jessica surrendered herself to the luxurious drifting sensation that suddenly took hold, buoying her above all her aches and pains, above all her cares, above all the remembered horrors of her day.

Much later, while she lay relaxing in a drug-induced euphoria, Jessica heard the distant sound of a door opening. Vaguely, she decided it was Jeff, returning safely from his meeting. Feeling wondrously happy, she decided her suspicions of dire consequences had been unnecessary.

The whispered voice she heard, though, wasn't Jeff's voice.

"Roman?" the voice repeated more insistently.

Then Roman's sleepy voice penetrated through her

haze. "A break-in at the museum, Mr. Whyte. That Billings guy's been shot."

Jessica tried desperately to come down from the clouds, but she was drifting, drifting, helplessly drifting. . .

4

"Jeff?" Jessica asked. Through how many hours of drug-induced slumber had she called his name?

"No."

Jessica managed to open her eyes and saw Dr. Changmai smiling at her. "Not, anyway, the last time I looked."

"Roman?" Jessica rolled over to check the next bed. The separating curtain was pulled only slightly, but enough for her to see the bed was empty.

"They say the third time is a charm, do they not?" Dr. Changmai encouraged, his smile growing wider.

"Dr. Changmai." Jessica slid up in bed feeling the worse for wear after her troubled sleep.

"Bingo! I was beginning to wonder there for awhile, but all's well that ends well. Speaking of 'well,' how are you feeling this morning?"

"I . . ." Jessica began. She wanted a verb, and she wasn't sure "dreamed" was the right one. "Was there anything in the morning news about a break-in at the Powell Whyte Museum?" she asked instead.

"No," Dr. Changmai replied, and if he found her question strange, he was apparently prepared to humor her. "Not that I recall. I'm sure I would have paid particular attention to something so extraordinary. We all rejoice at the return of our treasures to their rightful homeland. A break-in would undeniably be newsworthy."

"How about the shooting of an American?" She knew it could have been a dream. She hoped it was a dream. But she remembered hearing Nikolas and Roman so distinctly.

"The shooting of an American, or any foreigner, certainly would have made the news, too."

He seemed about to ask her what this was all about, so she headed him off at the pass. "Maybe I dreamt it."

"Ah!" He bobbed his head in agreement. "Most certainly a dream. Not uncommon in the aftermath of traumatic experiences. The mind sometimes lags behind the body in the healing process."

"But I dreamt of a break-in." It still didn't make sense to her. "I dreamt a friend was shot. None of it had anything to do with an explosion."

"Dreams often need extensive evaluation to decipher true meanings."

"It seemed so real." Jessica wished Roman were there so she could ask him what had happened. He'd know if Jeff had been shot.

"Fortunately, even the worst of our dreams are beneficial in sorting out the random thoughts that clutter our minds during our waking hours," the doctor continued in a maddeningly analytical tone. "Do you know that people who don't dream go quite mad? So, you must be thankful for your dreams and be assured their nightmarish quality will pale as the trauma that triggered them becomes further removed."

"I'll try to keep that in mind," Jessica promised. But despite the effects of her sedation, she knew she'd clearly heard voices in the night.

"So, aside from the dreaming, how are you?" Dr. Changmai lifted her eyelid and flashed his light at her pupil.

Jessica took a few seconds to isolate her aches and pains. "I've felt better, but considering everything I guess I'm all right."

Dr. Changmai moved his light to her other eye.

A few minutes later he clicked off the light and replaced it in the breast pocket of his pale blue hospital jacket.

"Your prognosis, doctor?" His continued cheerful demeanor made her hopeful.

"I really can't come up with any real reason to veto Roman's request to move you," said Dr. Changmai, "if he agrees to bring you back for a checkup in a week or so. Sooner if need be."

"Move me?"

"Of course, you should feel free to stay if you so prefer," Dr. Changmai offered with a twinkle in his eye. "Although if I were you, I'd be more inclined toward accommodations Roman might come up with."

He took her wrist and deftly located her pulse. Amazing the difference in touches, Jessica reflected. Neither Roman's touch nor the doctor's touch had affected her like Jeff's.

Had Jeff been shot during a break-in at the museum?

He'd wanted a look at the collection, because he suspected one of the recently arrived artifacts had been misplaced. Perhaps knowing his suspicions had planted seed that sprouted her macabre dream. Jeff would know the security at the museum was tight and designed to thwart professional art thieves. According to the terms of Powell Whyte's will, anything less than the best security could have compromised turning the complete collection over to Thailand. Jeff couldn't hope to penetrate such a high-tech system. On the other hand, how did a bodhisattva get misplaced under the scrutiny of all that sophisticated equipment?

"You've spoken to Roman recently then?" Jessica asked.

"Oh, yes," Dr. Changmai confirmed. "He called in and asked me to release you to his care. It's rather difficult to say no to such a generous patron of our hospital. Luckily, I'm not asked to go against my better medical judgment in obliging him on this one."

"You talked to him on the telephone?" Jessica tried not to make it sound like the third degree. "Do you know what time he left the hospital this morning?"

"No, but I suspect it was as soon as he was sure you were sleeping soundly. Sleeping on one of these beds usually requires sedation and even that doesn't always do the trick as you know."

He flashed Jessica a smile, which she returned.

"I *can* tell you when he's due back." Dr. Changmai glanced at his watch. "In approximately ten minutes. Which means I'd better get a nurse in here with your clothes if you're going to be ready." He headed for the door, stopped, and turned back. "The clothes you were wearing when you checked in were, I'm afraid, a bit worse for wear. At Roman's suggestion, I had one of our nurses pick up something to hold you over until you have access to your own things at the hotel."

"I seem to be a bit of a bother, don't I?"

"Nonsense!" Dr. Changmai argued. "It pleases us to do Roman a good turn on occasion. It doesn't make his generous patronage quite so one-sided."

"You're very gracious."

"And you're very kind to say so." Dr. Changmai bowed slightly and brought pyramided fingers briefly to his chin in salutation.

He left, replaced within seconds by Miss Chou, who appeared with a shopping bag. She laid out standard foundation garments, a simple blouse, wrap-around skirt, and rope sandals, finishing up with a mirror. "I hope I guessed the right sizes."

But Miss Chou turned out to have been right on the mark. Jessica doubted anyone, buying blind off the rack for someone else, could have done better.

"Thanks for everything, Miss Chou," Jessica said when she gave herself a final look in the mirror.

"Mr. Whyte is a very nice man," Miss Chou answered, as if that were thanks enough.

As if on cue, Roman stuck his head in the door. "Everyone decent?"

"Yes, we are decent." Miss Chou gathered up the mirror and now-empty shopping bag and pulled back the curtain which she'd closed around Jessica while she dressed. Smiling politely, Miss Chou greeted Roman and accepted Jessica's thanks before leaving the room.

"You look stunning, Miss Miller!" Roman said upon spotting Jessica seated on the edge of the bed.

Immediately, Jessica saw that Roman didn't look like

a man who'd been routed from his bed in the wee hours of
the morning to deal with a break-in and a shooting. He'd
obviously showered, shaved, and changed clothes. His
fresh suit was of ivory-colored raw Thai silk. There was a
small spray of green baby's-breath-like flowers in the
buttonhole of his jacket lapel. His cotton shirt was a cool,
pastel blue, whose button-down collar enclosed the loop of
his pale yellow tie. When he kissed her cheek, Jessica
noticed his cologne was different from the one he'd worn
before, but still no less complex in its combination of
exotic properties.

He took both her hands in his and stood back to look
at her. "How do you feel? Aside from the dreams Dr.
Changmai tells me you've been having."

"He told you, did he?" Jessica asked, feeling a little
ridiculous. By now, she knew she'd dreamed it all.

"He also told me such dreams are nothing to worry
about, and I agree with his diagnosis. Are you ready to
go?"

"Go where, exactly?" Jessica asked, although she
would welcome any change of scenery.

Roman narrowed his eyes and grinned mischievously.
"Four-nine-six Litchi Klong Road."

"That 'exactly' isn't what I meant."

"You'll like it," Roman promised, but before he could
say more, someone knocked on the door.

"All clear, Nikolas!" Roman called, and the door
opened to admit Nikolas and a wheelchair.

"I see some hospital procedures are universal." Jessica
welcomed a ride, this time around. She knew she was on
her way to a complete recovery, but she'd noticed while
dressing that she was still unsteady on her feet. She
managed the wheelchair without assistance, though, and

was soon on her way, Nikolas supplying momentum, Roman walking beside.

"Does the hospital have my forwarding address?" Jessica asked on their way to the front desk. "Jeff said he'd stop by or call back to see how I was doing."

"Does the lady think she's being spirited off with intent to keep her out of harm's — read that: Jeff Billings' — way?" Roman bantered, making Jessica blush. "Come on, now, Jessica," Roman cajoled lightheartedly, "what *do* you take me for?"

"Don't read anything into common courtesy that isn't there," Jessica insisted, and she felt like she was a kid caught with her hand in the cookie jar.

"You are a grown woman, are you not?" Roman teased. "Old enough to make your own decisions as regards your personal life and the people you want to let in it."

"And would you believe I'm starving?"

"Don't tell me the lady expects me to feed her, too?" Roman asked with mock horror, and Jessica rewarded him with a wide smile. She'd always appreciated his sense of humor. She couldn't imagine a marriage with any man who couldn't laugh at himself and make her laugh in turn.

Jeff, she knew, had a wonderful sense of humor.

Even when they'd been squashed down in that little coffin of a boat, a bullet hole gouged through the rotten wood, he'd made her laugh.

Where was Jeff now? If not dying of a bullet wound, was he at least safe after his two a.m. meeting?

"Risking triteness: a penny for your thoughts." Roman's light tone brought her back from her reverie. "Or, maybe a *baht*."

"My thoughts cost you nothing: I was thinking how

nice it is to have a good friend like you," which was true and she knew he wouldn't appreciate hearing that Jeff was on her mind.

"The feeling is mutual." His smile made her glad she hadn't reintroduced Jeff into their conversation. If Roman had remained a good sport about her inexplicable preoccupation with the author, she knew he couldn't condone what Jeff was doing in Bangkok. A lot of what Roman had, by way of worldly goods, came to him from his uncle, and it was logical he'd want to protect Powell Whyte's good name.

"Give a girl a break, Roman!"

"Not before I assure you of my impeccably good intentions," Roman insisted and stopped at the front desk. "We'll ask Miss Chou what instructions I left for *anyone* who should call for the missing Miss Miller."

"Miss Miller has checked out to four-nine-six Litchi Klong Road," said Miss Chou after checking an entry on a clipboard. "Telephone: six-four-three-two-two-one-six." She handed another clipboard with release forms to Jessica for signatures.

"Any special messages for a Mr. Billings, Miss Chou?" Roman asked slyly, and Jessica looked up to see that Miss Chou was without a clue.

"Roman!" Jessica shook her head as if he were amusing but incorrigible.

"Sorry, Miss Chou," Roman apologized, and, if Miss Chou didn't know why he was sorry, her smile said she appreciated it nonetheless.

Roman headed toward the front door, and Nikolas pushed Jessica along behind him.

The limousine was parked right outside, and Jessica felt five times better once she was inside it, with the wheelchair and the hospital receding behind her. She settled herself deeper into the rich-smelling, luxurious leather and decided it was good to be alive, even in a world where terrorists were intent upon making so many lives miserable.

"You know, this *was* really a marvelous idea," she told Roman, turning her head slightly to look at him.

"Thank you very much. I must say you look far better outside the sickroom environment."

So why couldn't Jeff be in Bangkok writing about someone — anyone — besides Powell Whyte?

Four-nine-six Litchi Klong Road: the home of Cecil and Betty Simms. "Off on their once-a-year holiday to visit the kids and grandkids in the States," Roman said. Jessica leaned on his arm as he guided her through the house to the spot prepared out back in the shade of a garden tamarind tree. Jessica had refused Roman, then Nikolas's offer to carry her. Nikolas, then, had disappeared somewhere, while three household servants — a cook, a maid, and a houseboy — hovered on the periphery. "The house was vacant," Roman explained, "and I said to myself, 'Wouldn't this be far better than a hospital room?' All it took was a quick phone call to arrange."

"I hope Cecil and Betty were understanding if you rooted them out of bed," Jessica said and found, now on her feet for longer than a few minutes, that she could manage surprisingly well.

"There's the time difference, don't forget."

The house and the garden, the latter ablaze with bougainvillea and flamboyants, surpassed even The Oriental Hotel as a setting most conducive to convalescence, and Jessica was thankful Roman had conceived the idea and the Simms's had graciously extended their hospitality.

"Cecil was in Thailand with Uncle Powell during World War II," Roman said.

Jessica and Roman were almost to the patio table and chairs, and Jessica figured his running dialogue was supposed to make her exercise seem less strenuous. Actually, Jessica enjoyed the return of her strength with every step.

"Cecil's in tin," Roman continued. "The mining of it," he added, as if she might misinterpret. "He met Betty in the Sixties when she came over with Bob Hope to entertain the troops headed for Nam. She'd just won Miss Something-or-Other. Miss California, I think."

If Betty were the attractive blonde in the evening gown and holding the parasol in the picture Jessica had spotted in the living room, the woman could certainly have been Miss Something-or-Other in the Sixties. If the photo were recent, the woman might still give some far younger contenders a run for their money.

"Cecil's hobby is architecture," Roman stopped next to a chair, complete with pillows and lap rug, the latter folded neatly over the arm until it was whipped out of the way by one of the ever-ready servants. "I think once you get a bit more strength, you'll enjoy seeing what he's done with this place."

"I certainly enjoy what I see so far," Jessica admitted. She had been in several Thai houses, and if this one might appear traditional to a novice, Jessica could spot the differences: the rooms connected by closed walkways, not by open breezeways; the stairway on the inside, not outside; the carved window frames faced inside, not outside. A classic Thai structure would be entirely unpainted, but although Cecil and Betty had left the inside walls natural teak, the outside was coated with the dull-red creosote introduced from England during the last century. Other anomalies were the modern bathroom, glimpsed by Jessica with real relief, the Italian marble that veneered the entrance way, and the Baccarat chandalier in the dining room.

"What you have here is a clever jigsaw of seven old houses Cecil had torn down and carted in from Pak Hai," Roman continued, making sure Jessica was comfortably settled. Once satisfied, he took the chair across the glass-topped table from her. "Of course, he's incorporated a few unique touches, like the carved partition between drawing room and the master bedroom which once graced the entry to a Bangkok pawn shop."

Jessica knew, even without the colorful preview, that she would enjoy a later, leisurely exploration. At the moment she was content to sit.

The servants faded into the woodwork, though Jessica knew they'd reappear the moment something needed to be done.

"Breakfast should be served shortly," Roman said.

"You mean you're going to feed me after all?" Jessica burrowed in the pillows, marveling at how the exquisite grounds isolated them from an outside world which wasn't far away. So much space devoted exclusively to trees and plants was a noticeable extravagance in a city as desperate for living space as Bangkok. It was only in such compounds as this, owned by very rich individuals or by very rich religious sects, or in the larger hotels that Jessica felt she saw this city as it must once have been. More than once, in the equally isolated garden at The Oriental Hotel, Jessica had conjured images of those earlier times when men and women indulged themselves shamelessly in quadrilles, waltzes, and polkas on well-manicured lawns.

"The klong's namesakes." Roman pointed to the row of evergreen trees that disguised the filthy and garbage-strewn canal and allowed only peeks of the water through breaks in the foliage. *"Nephelium Litchi,"* he identified, and Jessica thought of Litchi-nut-fruit, its thin, rough and brittle shell couching around a hard inner nut, a sweetly edible pulp that could challenge anything in deliciousness. "There used to be thousands such Litchi trees through here, but when Cecil bought this property, there wasn't a one left. He imported these from China."

Breakfast arrived and unlike the typical Thai breakfast of *kao tom*, which consisted of boiled rice soup with pork, chicken, or shrimp, this one made concessions to western tastes: orange juice; ham, cheese, and mush-room omelettes; hot, buttered scones; hot chocolate dotted with great dollops of decadent whipped cream, followed by papayas, pineapple, pomelo, tangerines, and bananas served in a polished wooden bowl.

"You know the old bit about the mountain coming to Mohammed?" Roman asked over the litter of their dessert. His blue eyes flashed the spatter of sunlight momentarily released through the weave of tamarind branches and leaves far overhead.

"That from a devout Mormon?" Jessica bantered with a smile. She leaned forward until their faces were only a short distance apart across the glass surface of the table. Once again, she realized Roman was one of the handsom-est men she'd ever known. But with a start she found she'd rather have Jeff sitting across the table from her.

"It just seemed apropos, since we've had to delay our original plans for today," he said cryptically.

Suddenly Jessica realized that she'd forgotten today was the day they were going to drive north. More importantly, she'd forgotten this was the day he'd promised . . . "Some good news connected with business!" she exclaimed.

"Therefore, observe the proverbial mountain." He removed the small spray of flowers from the buttonhole of his suit jacket. Jessica accepted the delicate stem that supported the minute green blossoms, and Roman identified them for her as expertly as he'd identified the trees along the klong: "*Goodera lipisin,*" he said. "A unique orchid variety once found only in a small patch of jungle outside Kumpu-wapi."

Jessica wasn't surprised that she held an orchid whose multiple, pinprick flowers were nothing like the large and fat-lipped blooms most popular at senior proms. She had an uncle with a green thumb who had explained, more than once, that a single flower family could come in infinite variations and forms.

Roman unfolded one of the fruit napkins on the tabletop. He took the spray of flowers from Jessica and laid it in the center of the cloth. He folded the linen over the flowers and applied a pulverizing pressure.

"And they were such pretty little things." Jessica would have grieved more, but she knew there must be some point inherent in their destruction.

"But any prettier than this?" He unfolded the linen so Jessica could see the result.

In dying, the crushed flowers made a luminescent green stain, and Jessica didn't know if she'd ever seen a lovelier shade of green. It was decidedly more full-bodied and glorious than the original green of the flowers.

"Seems a little old lady in a small village outside of

Kumpu-wapi eked out a living doing piecemeal
embroidery," Roman said. "She dyed her own threads,
using bark, moss, grass, and whatever, like her mother and
grandmother before her.

"Well, one of my companies happens to be Tompolin
Lumber, and about a year ago, we began clearing a tract of
forest land near Kumpu-wapi. We were a couple of weeks
into the operation when this little old lady turns up on our
doorstep and insists we stop cutting immediately because
we're on the verge of destroying her only source of a
particular green thread-dye. Luckily, I had a liaison on
hand who took the time to delve further. Not that the
woman was anxious to divulge the specifics of a family
secret guarded for generations. After all, there were several
other ladies in the village, out-and-out competition, who
had been trying to discover the secret source of the pretty
green dye. However, she told us when it was obvious we
wouldn't be stopped without something more concrete to
go on.

"Admittedly not *just* because of a desire to support a
cottage industry, I arranged for the few endangered
Goodera lipisin to be transplanted from the forest to a
controlled greenhouse environment. As a result, the old
woman no longer has to count on embroidery for survival,
and Whyte Silk Consortium has come up with this." From
inside his coat pocket, he produced a square of Thai silk.
The green smeared on the linen was nothing compared to
the way the radiant emerald fabric caught the available
light and danced like liquid in motion.

"Roman, it's lovely!" An expert on silk and Thai silk
in particular, Jessica knew the exceptional when she saw it,
and this was it. When she took the square from him and
felt how the sensuousness of silk seemed somehow

enhanced by the fluctuating shifts of the unique green color, she knew she'd never seen anything so exquisite.

"It took awhile to isolate the responsible chemical combination from the flowers available, but we finally found it and synthetically duplicated its magic," he said. "We still have a few minor problems to work out before we can produce in the volume we want, but we're projecting a start-up date about this same time next year. In the meantime, we happen to have the bolt of silk that resulted from the final stages of our experimentation. Granted, a mere hundred yards isn't much, compared to what we hope to soon make available, but it's yours if you'd like to buy it."

"You know I want to buy it!" Jessica knew she'd blown any chance of effecting a good bargain, but Roman knew her well enough to know he had her hooked. "The more pertinent question is whether or not I can afford it."

"Oh, I'm confident something can be worked out," he assured her. "Quite frankly, though I see this as giving you the business advantage, we see certain benefits in having the new dye introduced as part of a Jessica Miller collection. The dye isn't going to be inexpensive to produce, so we're aiming for an exclusive clientele. Namely, the people who buy Jessica Miller originals, or, more to the point, all of the haute couture designers like you, who cater to that rarified clothing market."

"You want to give me a ball-park figure on the bolt, so I can call home and mortgage the farm?"

"Why don't we just consider it yours?" Roman suggested. "We'll finalize the nitty-gritties after I get you north to see our lab and production facilities. I'm assuming, of course, that you still find behind-the-scenes as fascinating as ever."

"You assume right." Jessica knew designers who

avoided all the technical aspects of what produced a piece of cloth; the final result was all that mattered to them. But Jessica wasn't one of them. Everything she could learn about what went into making a particular bit of yardage helped her capture the magic of the material and translate it into a Jessica Miller original. Her success, especially with silks, proved she was doing something right. "When do we go?"

"When you're sure you're up to it," Roman told her. "I suspect it won't be too long if you don't overdo in the next twenty-four hours."

Jessica was about to argue she was up to the trip right then and there, but the houseboy arrived to announce her things had arrived from her hotel.

"Have Sen Tang put them away," Roman said.

Jessica knew she wouldn't be able to persuade either Roman or any accommodating servant that she could do it herself.

"In the meantime, bring me those pencils and drawing pads I had sent around for Miss Miller," Roman instructed. When the boy hurried off, Roman turned back to Jessica with a smile. "I suspected you might get a bit stir crazy, sitting around doing nothing, so I figured you might like the time to think up ways to use those hundred yards of green silk."

"Did anyone ever tell you you were psychic?" Jessica was indeed anxious to put pencil to paper. Almost without realizing it, the news of the new dye had sparked several creative images that were crying to be put down on paper. Besides, work for her had always been as much a catharsis as tears, and she needed all the help she could get to void the damage of these last few hours.

"Idle hands are the devil's workshop, or some other

such suitable bit of wisdom," Roman said as the houseboy returned with sketch pads, pencils, and telephone.

"A phone call for you, Mr. Whyte," the boy told Roman.

In spite of herself Jessica felt a stab of disappointment that it wasn't Jeff calling her. At the same time she chided herself for too much preoccupation with Jeff Billings. Here she was, just made privy to an exciting new dye that could make her next show a real standout, and she superfluously cluttered her mind with how Jeff said he'd check in but hadn't.

Roman finished his brief phone conversation with an, "Okay, I'll come over now and go over the figures with you." He replaced the receiver but stopped the houseboy from taking the phone. "I think Miss Miller might prefer it left out here, Chai." He turned to Jessica. "I thought you might want to call Nora."

"Yes, I do," Jessica agreed. If Jessica were on her way to recovery, the horror of the bombing already blessedly dream-like, Nora had Tim's death to keep the memory alive. Jessica felt a little guilty that life, for her, had begun to feel so good again.

"I have Nora's number." Roman removed a folded piece of paper from his pocket. "Dealing with Bangkok operators, even to finagle a simple phone number, isn't the rest and relaxation the doctor ordered."

Then he stood. "Business has a perverse way of messing up enjoyable social occasions. If you need me, my number is the one written just below Nora's. Even if you don't need me, I've still invited myself to supper."

Jessica watched him leave, and she fondled the smooth green silk he'd left behind. Again, the sensuousness of it triggered mental images of design possibilities.

She put the swatch to one side for future reference and unfolded the piece of paper Roman had given her.

She picked up the phone and dialed Nora Spencer.

Jessica didn't recognize the voice through the static on the phone line, although it sounded familiar. It wasn't Nora, but that didn't surprise her. The Relief Society was fast to give a helping hand.

"Hello, this is Jessica Miller."

"Jessica! Sheila Phao."

"Sheila, of course," Jessica blamed the continuing noise on the line for not identifying the soft-spoken Thai weaver right off. "How's Nora?"

"She seems to be handling it pretty well," Sheila said. Then, she dropped her voice to almost a whisper. "It's hard to tell. I've seen the ones who seem to have it most together come apart at the seams." Her voice returned to normal: "By the way, how are you? I called the hospital this morning, and they said you'd checked out to convalesce at — Hold on! —four-nine-six Litchi Klong Road?"

"Some friends of Roman Whyte graciously loaned me their place while they're out of town," Jessica confirmed, delighted the hospital was passing on her address. Had she even momentarily suspected that Roman and Miss Chou had joined forces to keep her whereabouts a secret?

"I have a telephone number for you, too," Sheila informed. "Six-four-three-two-two-one-six?"

"That's it," Jessica confirmed, after simultaneously checking the numbers against those listed on the base of the phone.

"I tried to get through a few minutes ago, but the line was busy," Sheila said. "Are you up to visitors, or would you rather. . . ." She stopped to say to someone on her end of the line: "Jessica Miller." Her voice came back full in

Jessica's ear: "I'll turn you over to Nora, Jessica, and check with you later."

"Jessica?" Jessica didn't know if Nora's voice was distorted by grief or by the infuriating static. "Jessica?" Nora repeated, as if she doubted her opening had made it through the noise.

"Is there anything I can do, Nora?" Jessica asked, and, once again, she gave thanks that she hadn't shared Tim's fate when the bomb had exploded in the restaurant. "You know how sorry I am, and my prayers are with you."

"Everything seems under control," Nora judged, and Jessica thought the woman sounded pretty much herself. "The Relief Society has been marvelous, and Charlotte is flying in from Boston tomorrow. Did you ever meet my daughter?"

"No." Jessica vaguely remembered just missing Charlotte and her husband on her last time through Bangkok.

"Her husband is a Professor of Literature at Boston University," Nora said. To Jessica it sounded like an attempt at continued small talk.

"I suppose I shouldn't keep you." Jessica knew from personal experience that there were things to do when a loved one died that couldn't be done by someone else, no matter how well-meaning that someone else might be.

"I've decided to take Tim to Seattle," Nora said. If she were anxious for Jessica to ring off, she gave no indication. "Most of his family is there. There'll probably be some kind of memorial service here, but I can't say for sure until Charlotte arrives. She's better in a crisis than I am. I remember when Grandma Spencer died. . . ." She stopped, as if recalling something once forgotten and asked, "How about you, Jessica? I hear it's only a miracle you're still alive."

"Bruises, aches, and pains." Considering Nora's wound caused by Tim's death, Jessica almost felt guilty that she couldn't have something a bit more major to report.

"So many innocent people hurt, maimed, or killed," Nora said with a sigh. "Of course, the terrorists didn't consider Tim an innocent. And, that's why they killed him. Anyway, that's what the man said over the radio before anyone had told me officially that my husband was dead."

"Nora, that's a horrible way to find out!"

"Actually, over the radio, or over TV, was the way I'd always imagined I'd hear," Nora admitted. "So, when it did happen that way, I said to myself, 'Well, Nora, there it is, then.' And you know, along with grief, there was the undeniable relief that I wasn't going to be put through any more years of waiting for it to happen."

Jessica knew talking things through was a time-proven catharsis, so she let Nora talk. Possibly Nora found it easier to unburden herself to Jessica, on the other end of an inanimate phone, than to any of the sisters there with her.

"I think Tim was expecting something like this to happen," Nora said. "Oh, probably not there in the Normandie Room, but sometime soon. I might not always have known the specifics of the job he was working on, but I could always tell when things weren't going well. And this job wasn't. Others might have been fooled by his easy-going facade, his quick smile, and his jokes, but he couldn't fool me. When he told Clarence that some guy from Montana was a ticking time bomb waiting to blow them all up, I got this funny feeling."

"Clarence *West*?" Jessica asked, just because it was

something to say.

"You knew him?" Nora asked and sounded surprised. "He'd only just arrived."

"I met him once, and only briefly." Jessica decided it was neither the time nor the place to explain the circumstances.

"Poor Clarence," Nora said. "The terrorists didn't consider him an innocent, either. 'Two capitalist pigs in one poke,' is how the terrorist spokesman put it. I suppose that's his version of, 'Two birds with one stone.'"

Jessica waited for Nora to continue, but when it became evident the women had pretty much said all she felt up to saying, she took her cue and signed off.

Jessica had just hung up the phone, her hand still curled around the receiver, when it rang, making her jump. Startled, she took a deep breath to settle her suddenly pounding heart, and the phone rang twice more.

When the phone was still unanswered on its fourth ring, the houseboy stuck his head out the back door of the house. Jessica waved her hand in dismissal and picked up the receiver.

"Six-four-three-two-two-one-six," she read off the phone number noncommittally.

"Jessica Miller?"

5

She recognized his voice, even if she'd never seen the man. There was no forgetting it or him. She might hear him in a million years, and she would still have his voice down pat. It was the man who'd called her on the pay phone!

"You!"

"They told me where you were when I called the hospital," he replied. "I was sorry to hear about your accident but happy you were far enough away from the blast to survive. Speaking of which, don't you think a thank-you is in order?"

"A thank-you?" Jessica asked, aghast. "Do you know how many people you murdered and maimed in that blast?"

"Me?" he asked and sounded genuinely surprised. "Oh, I see!" he added in apparent insight. "You think I planted the bomb, and then out of some sense of chivalry, called you at the last minute to remove you from harm's way? Wrong, Miss Miller! I no more set that bomb than I fired the rifle at you and Mr. Billings."

What was the nagging sensation suddenly spawned inside her that intuitively said she'd just been given a jigsaw piece she could fit easily into place if she just concentrated long enough to make the necessary connection?

"Just because it was pure accident that I called last night when I did," he continued, "it did save your life, didn't it?"

"So, thank you for that," Jessica conceded. "Now, what do you want this time?"

"The same thing I wanted last time," he told her. "I have a package I'd like very much to sell to Mr. Billings."

Once again Jessica felt as if she were a cryptographer with cipher and key but still unable to decipher some sort of hidden message. What was this man trying to tell her? And how much of it was other than it seemed?

"I would have thought Jeff gave you the answer to your proposal when he met you this morning," Jessica said. "Anyway, he certainly gave me the impression that was one of the first things on his agenda."

There was a pregnant silence, and Jessica thought she'd lost him.

"What meeting this morning?" he asked as she was about to query if he were still on the line.

"Jeff left me at the hospital at two this morning," Jessica told him, although she suspected it was superfluous information, as far as this mystery man was concerned. "He said he was going to see you."

Or had he said any such thing? In reality, hadn't it been Jessica who'd told Jeff whom he was going to see?

Hadn't Jeff acted surprised to hear her notion that he was off to meet the man she'd talked to on the pay phone?

"I didn't meet with Jeff Billings this morning," the voice informed her in no uncertain terms, and Jessica experienced a tremor in the pit of her stomach. "If he told you otherwise, he's lying."

As Jessica scurried to think of some retort, she was saved by a new outburst of static, followed closely by an unexpected exclamation from her unidentified caller.

"You think I wouldn't be clever enough to know your phone is bugged!" he accused loudly. "Why is your phone bugged?"

Jessica heard the distinctive click as he broke their connection. Then, after a fraction of a second, she heard another click, followed by the return of a dial tone. She recognized the sequence from TV detective shows: someone talking on the phone, the connection broken, the additional click before dial tone. It was always the clue for Thomas Magnum, or Rick and A.J. Simon, or Amanda King to unscrew the mouthpiece and find the bug someone had planted there.

Of course, this wasn't a movie or a detective series, and her caller's accusation was stuff and nonsense. He was obviously paranoid, which was why he kept calling her when it was Jeff he wanted to see.

It hit her then that the certain something that triggered inside of her every time she'd heard the man say Jeff's name. It also went back to what Nora had said about the guy from Montana who was a time bomb waiting to go off. *Billings* was Jeff's last name, but it was also a town in Montana.

However, was Jessica going off the deep end when she tried to equate the Billings in Jeff with the Billings in

Montana, just because of something Nora might have heard Tim tell Clarence West?

Jessica picked up the phone, pulled the paper with Nora's number over to her, and began to dial. She'd ask if Tim said "Billings" or "Montana." And, how would she ever explain her need to know that to Nora?

Halfway through her dialing, there was a spurt of static, and Jessica disconnected. She hadn't heard the two distinct, telltale clicks before the return of the dial tone, but she knew what she was going to do.

She unscrewed the mouthpiece.

"Don't get carried away," she told herself. "You are probably seeing spooks where they don't exist. Your mind is still a little scrambled from the explosion, right? What possible connection could Jeff Billings have with Tim Spencer? And who would want to bug your phone?"

She lifted the telephone's innards from the plastic mold that contained them. The dime-sized disk was left behind.

She'd never seen a listening device, except on television and in the movies, but she knew one when she saw one. And the reality of this one, being where it was, injected a whole new dimension into recent events.

Was it only two days ago that her life was normal and predictable? When had things gotten out of control? How deep was the intrigue into which she had suddenly fallen? She wasn't sure she wanted to know the answers, but she knew they involved Roman. Roman had brought her here, seemingly on the spur of the moment. But the phone was bugged. Why?

Was Roman just interested in what Jeff might say to Jessica about the progress of research on Powell Whyte? That could explain how readily Roman left Jessica's new address and telephone number at the hospital. Or had Roman done it purely to protect Jessica from someone he considered a bad influence? If so, he had to know she'd never condone such a blatant violation of her privacy. Of course, there was the possibility he never dreamed she'd find out. She shuddered as the implications of that raced through her mind. As she removed the bug and put the phone back together, she began to shake. The tiny electronic listening device frightened her as much as being shot at, or narrowly escaping a bombing. She felt out of her depth, as if she'd suddenly been thrown into a sea of horror with no rescue in sight.

She did know what to do with the bug, though. She'd seen Thomas Magnum run one over with a red Ferrari, Rick Simon crunch one beneath his scuffed boot, and Amanda King drop one in a simmering pot of chili.

Jessica tossed this one into the Litchi trees and listened expectantly for a splash in the filth-contaminated klong. Instead, she heard it richochet off a tree trunk.

Jessica sat there, miserable, tempted to call Roman and vent her anger. However, since he was scheduled to join her for supper, she decided she'd confront him face to face. She wanted to read his expression when she asked him what was going on. She didn't want him to disconnect and blame the Bangkok phones, thereby having time to come up with some story other than the truth.

It suddenly struck her that she should have kept the bug as evidence. What did she say when a confronted Roman said, in all innocence, "Bug, what bug?"

She decided to retrieve it. It was there somewhere. It might be small, but it was shiny, and that would help her find it.

She got up, and the phone rang again. Hesitantly she

picked it up.

"Jessica, Jeff," came the unexpected greeting.

Was she happy to hear his voice? Was she angry? Was she relieved? Was she afraid? She was beset by all those conflicting emotions, but Jeff didn't give her even a moment to sort them.

"I want you to help me arrange a meeting with Roman, Jessica," he said, his voice clear on the static-free phone. "I'd prefer not to involve you, but I want to know why Roman sent a gunman to shoot me at the museum this morning, and you're the one go-between we both know. One I hope we can both trust."

Jessica had plenty of questions, but Jeff gave her no chance to ask them, let alone get answers. Then, as if he read her mind, he said, "There's no time for questions now, Jessica, because I don't want to trust the phone any longer than necessary."

"Don't worry, I've de-bugged it," she said dryly.

"No kidding!" His tone seemed to imply what would a dress designer know about electronic surveillance? "That's good news. Are you up and about?"

"I can take a few steps but don't ask me to dance any jigs."

"A few steps are all that are necessary," he assured her. "Just take them at three o'clock this afternoon down toward the Litchi trees. I'll have a boat waiting to take you across the klong. With luck, you'll be across before anyone can follow."

"Follow?" Jessica echoed hollowly.

"Roman is probably having you watched," Jeff explained.

"I thought you wanted to meet with Roman," she said. "What does sending a boat for me have to do with that?"

"You and I need to talk first," he told her. "I want your help, but I want you to feel right about helping me. When you hear what I have to say, face to face, you can judge for yourself. For all I know, you might not believe I've been wounded until you see the bullet hole."

Since his complaint of a wound verified what Jessica thought she'd heard Nikolas relay to Roman at the hospital, Jeff had more chance of her believing that, here and now, than he had of convincing her she should run off somewhere to meet him at three o'clock.

"Why would Roman think you'd contact me at all?"

"Maybe intuition. Or maybe he heard me say I'd check back in with you, and he took me for a man of my word. Maybe he knew a wounded man would be desperate for an understanding ear and a friendly face."

Instinctively she knew she could trust Jeff, but she also knew Roman could no sooner have masterminded a shoot-out with Jeff at the museum than Jessica could sing "Aida."

"Jessica?"

"Yes, Jeff?"

"If you decide not to meet me, I *will* understand."

The phone went dead. Not two clicks this time: just one and the dial tone.

Jessica replaced the receiver and waited for the phone to ring again. When it didn't, she sat back and breathed a sigh of exasperation.

What did she do now? Rendezvous with someone shot while breaking into the museum? If he *had* been breaking in, since "breaking in" was how Nikolas had put it, and, undoubtedly, Jeff would call it something else. If it had been clear-cut breaking in, why the cover-up, with no word in the press, while Roman and Dr. Changmai allowed her to think she'd dreamed Nikolas's announcement?

How was Jessica to handle the possibility of Jeff as "the man from Montana," as mentioned by Tim Spencer to Clarence West, as overheard by Nora? Jessica could think of other places she'd rather be than with a time bomb waiting to blow a second time.

On the other hand, it would be nice to see if Jeff had the answers to some of the questions Jessica would like to ask him, and he deserved a chance to tell her his side of the story.

Last, but not least, the phone *had* been bugged, which told her Jeff had every right to be paranoid. And so did she.

Jessica wondered what Roman would have made of her conversation with Jeff? Roman could have intercepted the boat if his sole concern were Jessica's safety. Or, if Jeff were the one he wanted, he could have tried to follow Jessica to Jeff.

Jessica stood and tested her legs. Almost simultaneously, the houseboy stuck his head inside the door. "Anything wrong, Miss Miller?" Jessica didn't know whether he was genuinely concerned or had been instructed by Roman to make sure she didn't try to hop any boats Jeff might send for her on the klong.

"I need a bit of exercise," she told him. Granted, Dr. Changmai hadn't told her to walk marathons, but he hadn't told her to stay immobile. A compromise seemed a fitting solution for good health, especially if she were to be limber enough for a three o'clock boat ride.

She strolled slowly around the garden, periodically glancing toward the house to see what the servants were up to. They'd all disappeared from sight, but Jessica bet if she called for a lemonade, the houseboy would materialize in a flash. What's more, lemonade sounded good enough to keep in mind for when she finished her reconnaissance.

She pictured how it would be at three o'clock if she bypassed flower arbors, skirted well-trimmed shrubs, slipped through the Litchi trees, and embarked on the awaiting boat. Mid-klong, she'd glance back and spot the frustrated houseboy on the shore.

"Sounds like a scenario from a B movie," Jessica said to herself. "Not just the chase scene, but my whole life these last couple of days."

She'd been in Bangkok numerous times before, and nothing like this had happened. So why this time? Jeff Billings: that was why! Everything else, everyone else, were constants; Jeff the only variable. Therefore, it could logically be concluded Jeff made Bangkok the place Jessica could never view quite so innocently again. She wasn't sure she could forgive him for tainting her vision, even if she might have been looking at it through rose-colored glasses.

She tried to clear her mind and give it a rest. She focused her concentration on the beauty and fragrance of a flowering frangipani. The tree was as much an indication of the foreign owners of this compound as was the modern bathroom inside the house. Although the tree was often found in Buddhist temples, a Thai would never dream of growing one at home. The Thai name for frangipani was *lantome*, which sounded similar to *ratome*, a Thai word for "heartbroken." Roman had told Jessica that bit of trivia during one of their many strolls through Bangkok. Could the man who stopped beneath a flowering frangipani to bend down a flower-heavy branch so Jessica could better examine and smell the radiant fragrance of snow-white blossoms? Could that man bug the telephone and cover up the shooting of Jeff at the museum?

She marveled at her mind's quick sidestep from innocent frangipani to the troubles she was trying to forget.

She stopped at the Litchi trees. Of course, it was too early for Jeff's boat, but she remembered she planned to search for the bug. The rotting odor of the klong rose from the water and invaded the peace of the garden. After a few minutes Jessica decided no evidence was worth subjecting herself to the smell and retreated to the surprisingly fresh air around the table.

Immediately, the houseboy appeared with silver tray, Baccarat glass and pitcher, the latter filled halfway with lemonade.

"You read my mind!" Jessica exclaimed. Actually, his foresight made her a little uneasy. She preferred not to be second-guessed so easily. Then again, the day was hot, Jessica had puttered around the garden, and servants knew lemonade was a favorite thirst-quencher the world over. So she graciously accepted the cool liquid and enjoyed. She didn't even bother to ask if he'd used water from a bottle.

When the houseboy didn't disappear as quickly as he appeared, Jessica looked up. "Cook wants to know if a cold pasta salad would suit for lunch," he said.

"It would suit just fine." Jessica wondered if it could possibly be lunch time. She desperately needed a watch to replace the one broken during the sniper incident. "And," she stopped the houseboy in his retreat," "could you please check to see if anyone came across my travel clock when my things from the hotel were unpacked?"

In no time she had her clock and the correct time: 10:45 a.m. After that, time dragged, despite the distraction of lunch and Jessica's various attempts to sketch. She was particularly perturbed that she couldn't regain the original spurt of creative adrenaline released by her first contact with the swatch of green silk. Oh, the designs she came up with weren't to be sneezed at. She even imagined that Henry Smythe-Wilson would be glad to have them since, as soon as Jessica had left his salon to go out on her own, his business had undergone a slump from which it had never really recovered. But the designs weren't Jessica's best efforts, and she knew it. They weren't the something special that the green silk demanded to supplement its sensuous beauty. If Jessica were out *just* to turn heads, the silk could do that on its own. What she wanted to do, what she had to do, was turn this bit of luck into a real fashion statement: a convergence of silk and design that screamed, 'This is what a Jessica Miller original is all about!'

"I didn't need any of the distractions of the past two days!" she said aloud.

At 2:45 she dropped her sketch pad on the glass-top table with a thud.

"I'm a designer and a good one. I didn't come to Bangkok to be embroiled in mystery and intrigue. I didn't come to figure out who shot whom, and why; who bombed whom, and why. I didn't come to be shot at and blown up. I came to buy silk, maybe have a good time, enjoy a few good meals, and renew relationships with friends and acquaintances. Do I care if Powell Whyte exploited Thai resources and swiped Thai art treasures? Do I care how Roman and Jeff are involved in Powell Whyte activities? Powell Whyte is dead and buried."

Of course, Jessica knew Powell Whyte had been the victim of a still unsolved murder. Remembering that gave her a disconcerting chill.

"Undoubtedly, another can of worms!" she decided.

She retrieved her sketch pad and pencil and tried once again for inspiration. In the end, she surrendered to the inevitable and settled back with a sigh, sketch pad forgotten in her lap.

Unfortunately, whether she liked it or not, her life was no longer the same. For better or worse, Jeff Billings had changed it forever. What Jessica had to do was survive the change, adjust to it, make it work for her. After all, she'd never lived in a vacuum. Nor did she get where she was by not giving as good as she got. She was a surviver, and she would survive this.

Well, she'd survive if she could just figure out the game, the stakes, and all the players.

At 2:59, Jessica got up, expecting the houseboy to come running. When he didn't, she was a little disappointed. A part of her wanted an excuse to miss her rendezvous with the boat on the klong. That she was going at all had a lot to do with her first impressions of Jeff, which had been positive ones, enhanced by the way he'd responded so protectively during the sniper incident, coupled by his concern when he'd visited her at the hospital. Her life would have been so much easier if she'd taken one look and immediately judged him a crook, a liar, and a scoundrel. Then she could have sided with Roman one hundred percent and not felt somehow disloyal by so generously giving Jeff the benefit of the doubt. It would have helped, of course, if she hadn't overheard Nikolas tell Roman at the hospital about the shooting, and if she hadn't found that wretched listening device in the phone.

If nothing else, Jeff might suggest some viable answers, and that would make the meeting worthwhile. If she didn't swallow what he tried to feed her, she'd just tell him she didn't want any part in helping him.

Although she was loathe to admit it, she also wanted to see Jeff just to see him. She didn't believe in the mysterious electricity Roman had mentioned seeing, but she had to admit she was attracted to him. No, she didn't want to think about *that* until she knew where Jeff was coming from.

Just to make sure she wasn't telegraphing any obvious signals which would bring the servants racing from the house, she paused momentarily by a small tree of scarlet hibiscus. Almost immediately, she wished she hadn't. Not because anyone apparently noticed and considered it suspect, but because of a Thai superstition that said the showy red flowers were unlucky because they'd once been worn behind the ears of Thai executioners.

Nervously, Jessica checked her wrist for a watch that still wasn't there. She didn't want to arrive at the klong early, or the boat wouldn't be there; she didn't want to arrive late or someone might spot the boat before she boarded and wonder about it. Jessica had never been all that good at counting seconds.

Without further ado, she made directly toward the Litchi trees and smelled the klong even before she stepped through the shrubbery to the water's edge.

Apparently her timing couldn't have been better, because the boat glided into place the moment she got there.

"Quickly, please!" the Thai boatman insisted. Actually, boat*boy* might have been more apropos, because he didn't look a day over ten. Like his small boat, which was far smaller than the small water taxi on the Chao Phraya, his clothes were of a shade exactly matching the contaminated russet of the canal.

Deftly, Jessica boarded, and the small craft angled downstream toward the opposite embankment. No motor on this boat, and she suspected noise was the deciding factor. The kid had a single paddle which he dipped silently to one side of the boat and then to the other.

Jessica sat in the cramped bow and faced the boatman and the receding shoreline. While in her earlier fanciful conjurations of this scene she'd pictured the houseboy in hot pursuit, there was no sign of him now. Which made the escape anticlimactic.

"Oh, well," she·said to herself, "thus it is that daydreams differ from reality." However, the thought was hardly past when there was the distinct sound from the bank of a bear barreling through the brush, accompanied by a bellowing that raised gooseflesh and put the militant screams of Rambo to shame. It wasn't the houseboy who appeared through the shrubbery, but Roman's bodyguard, Nikolas. But he didn't stop his forward momentum when confronted by the klong. In a thoroughly graceful dive, the kind Olympic racers used to hit the water in a skimming glide, Nikolas kept right on coming.

Jessica couldn't believe her eyes. She was held absolutely spellbound by this man who'd entered the equivalent of an open-air sewer and had proceeded from there as if he were sprint-training in a private pool.

Jessica wasn't the only one who found the sight unusual. Her boatman had turned back at the noise and was still turned to watch in fascination. His paddling had been completely interrupted in the process.

A small current to keep the boat on course, but it was nothing compared to the progress Nikolas made. Within a surprisingly short period of time, the man had covered half the distance between shoreline and boat.

Suddenly, the young boatman came to life, obviously spurred on by the sudden shouts aimed at him from the opposite shore.

"Chawla! Chawla!" came screams from Jessica's back, and she figured they were either calling the boatman's name or something that meant "get a move-on!" In any event, they spurred him out of his lethargy. He returned to work with a vengeance while Jessica continued to watch Nikolas's impressive progress. In Jessica's estimation, the boatman's best efforts would be hard-pressed to get them to the far shore before Nikolas reached them.

This wasn't the first time Jessica had seen someone brave the contaminated waters of the Bangkok klongs. But it was the first time she'd seen a European attempt a feat that would have given Houdini second thoughts. It all went back to those generations of immunities built up within populations indigenous to an area. Thai children might swim these klongs safely today because their fathers, grandfathers, and great grandfathers swam and bathed in them. But Nikolas wasn't Thai, and if his system hadn't accumulated more than its share of immunities from his fighting as a mercenary in wars that took place amid environments possibly more germ-ridden than these waters, the man had to be crazy.

His well-coordinated body, the rhythmic pulls of his muscled limbs, held her spell-bound. She found it marvelous the way his body sliced the reddish brown scum and gave a strangely intoxicating beauty to water odious and ugly without it. It robbed her precarious situation of urgency.

The boatman, though, and his cheering section on shore, continued their strongest efforts until the time the bow of the boat hit the embankment, and Jessica felt the jolt.

"Please, please!" the boatman screamed as he discarded his paddle and came forward to step on Jessica's foot. However, not even the pain from his weight on her instep drew her attention from the streamlined Nikolas.

Suddenly, a pair of hands grabbed her and roughly jerked her from the boat. "This way, Miss Miller! Faster! Faster!" Supported between two men while the boatman ran off in another direction, she was literally lifted off the ground and carried to a taxi parked on the road just off the klong. Motivated by their demands, she hurried toward the car. Hesitating briefly at the open door, the sun glinted on the shiny metal of a gun.

"In!" commanded a man she'd never seen before. He reached for her arm with his free hand while the two men who still held her shoved her forward. "On the floor! On the floor!" the man repeated.

Three pair of hands pushed and prodded her into place, the door slammed shut behind her, and something heavy and musty enveloped her.

She was furious, battered, and indignant. And scared. Her position was awkward and cramped. The smells of oil, gas, sweat, and garlicky breath assaulted her. The taxi burned rubber as it pulled out, adding the acrid stench of latex and thick dust to the already disagreeable melange.

And where was Jeff? Had he canned her? Or had these men done something to him? No, this had to be his plan, but why?

6

Near the point of panic, Jessica concentrated on remembering Jeff's telephone call. She didn't think she'd misread him. Jeff had, afterall, been unfairly shot at the museum and therefore had every reason to take stringent precautions not to let it happen a second time.

However, if Jeff were right, Roman was the villain of the piece and somewhere down the line Jessica had been wrong in her assessment of him — and that just didn't seem possible, either. So who had bugged her phone?

While mentally debating all those frustrating quandaries, the man in the cab said, "Please listen carefully, Miss Miller. In a very short time this car will stop, and I'll remove the blanket that covers you. You are to sit up, get out of the cab, and enter the taxi parked directly beside this one. Is that perfectly clear?"

"Is all this really necessary?" Jessica asked caustically,

wondering if her body would ever recover from all it had been put through these last couple of days.

"Do you understand the instructions?" the man repeat, ignoring her sarcasm.

"Yes." Jessica rallied at the prospect of getting off the grubby floor, even if she were merely transferred to another equally grubby one.

"In this other taxi, there will be a blanket on the backseat. You will get on the floor and immediately cover yourself with the blanket. Is that clear?"

'Couldn't I sit on the seat?"

"No, and yes, this is all necessary. Or, at least I deem it so, and someone has paid very well for my expertise in this matter."

"Jeff paid you, you mean?" Jessica asked, but her stomach knotted at the thought that this might have been engineered by someone else. But she knew she could not have mistaken anyone else for Jeff on the phone that morning.

"Just follow instructions, Miss Miller," the man said. "I assure you, you'll come through with flying colors."

The taxi made a sharp right that took Jessica off guard. She still searched for her sense of balance when the taxi stopped.

The covering came off, the back door came open, but she stayed where she was, lost in a kind of daze that told her she wasn't really playing discarded pretzel on a smelly car floor.

"This way, please."

Identifying the voice of the man in the cab, she looked toward the open door, and there he was. His salt-and-pepper hair and beard looked like glued-on steel wool. His suit was brown, soiled, and at least two sizes too big.

Without his drawn gun, though, he looked far less menacing. As he helped her out into an almost deserted warehouse, he wasn't nearly as rough as when he'd yanked her inside the cab. Maybe that was because Nikolas wasn't in such visibly hot pursuit.

Using a modified backward crawl, Jessica eased her way out of the car. There were oily spots on the black material of her skirt which she tried unsuccessfully to brush away.

"Your delivery service leaves much to be desired."

In response the man merely gestured her to the second car. She half expected him to shove her in, but he waited while she assumed her own position on the floor. At least this time she could contrive a more comfortable ride. Reluctantly, she pulled a blessedly clean blanket off the seat and put it over her.

Immediately the car started, pulling forward amid a cacophony of metal grating against metal. Jessica hoped the noises were a warehouse door opening, because if it were the taxi, she figured they were in big trouble.

Once on the way, knowing only the driver shared the car with her, Jessica felt far braver. In fact, she contemplated throwing off the cover, opening the door, and making her escape. The noises now coming to her, accompanied by the slow, start-and-stop progress of the car, said she was somewhere with lots of people and traffic. However, with escape now such a viable option, it seemed less the necessity. Maybe she was headed for Jeff after all. Since she'd come this far, it would be ridiculous to pull out before she got any return on her substantial physical and mental investment.

Aside from the unorthodox seating arrangement and the shroud of a blanket that made the interior intolerably hot and humid, she was still determined not to call it quits when the car stopped and she was told, "Uncover, please!"

She threw back the blanket and half expected to see Jeff, but instead there was only the driver's pockmarked face.

"Into the dress shop, please," he said.

"What dress shop?" Jessica asked and, weak-kneed, scrambled to see where he was pointing.

They were parked on a Bangkok street typically cluttered with sidewalk stalls and masses of foot traffic. The driver of a car blocked by the taxi honked his horn impatiently and screamed for the driver of the taxi to get the vehicle out of the way.

"Tell the clerk you've come from Mr. Montana, please," Jessica's keeper said, leaning over the seat to open the back door from the inside.

"Mr. Montana?" Jessica asked quizzically. She shivered at the thought that Mr. Montana had any connection with the man from Montana mentioned by Tim Spencer to Clarence West.

She got out and felt more than a little wobbly and shopworn. No one would ever dream this grease-stained ragamuffin designed clothes for some of the world's wealthiest and most elegant women. Or was that the whole point?

With a bit of pulling and tugging to reposition her skirt, Jessica entered the small dress shop located between a butcher shop and a fish market whose lines of dead fish with milky eyes did little to lift Jessica's flagging spirits.

Just inside the shop, Jessica spotted a black wrap-around skirt that could, for a few *bahts*, replace the one she wore. However, the prospects of even lousier accommodations to come discouraged her from making the effort.

A little old lady occupied a chair set so deeply among the clothing that Jessica almost missed her. Hoping for the end of her miserable journey, Jessica approached her. "I'm from Mr. Montana."

"Back door, there," the old woman indicated with a shaky finger.

"Right." Out the back door was the alley. In the alley was a tuk tuk. On the tricycle end of the tuk tuk was another seemingly ageless Thai who could have been six or sixty. Well, Jessica thought, maybe that was a slight exaggeration, especially as the man's bass-voiced, "See the sights, miss?" confirmed he'd long ago reached puberty.

"Sure," Jessica said, after first assessing that all other offers were nonexistent.

She climbed into the rickshaw portion of the tuk tuk and luxuriated in the comparison between it and the cabs she'd ridden in to get there. She leaned back, stretched her legs, and as soon as the tuk tuk entered the main thorough-fare, Jessica spotted the Royal Hotel straight ahead. The hotel was the only reference point Jessica needed to pinpoint her location and direction: she was headed west on Rajadamnern Klang, and there was no greater balm for her frazzled nerves. As the tuk tuk turned left onto Ratchadamnoen Nai, the Pramane Ground, where they held the weekend market, she was almost her old self again. After spending so much time under a blanket, even the present heat and humidity of the Bangkok afternoon seemed less oppressive than usual.

Soon they were parallel to the golden spires, and decorative pavilions of the Buddhist Wat Phra Keo. Her driver pulled to a stop in front of one gate. "There's still time for you to see the Emerald Buddha, miss."

Jessica realized suddenly that she didn't have any money in her pockets. She got out of the tuk tuk and walked slowly away from it, at any moment expecting the driver to shout that she was trying to cheat him out of his fare. When she reached the gate, she looked back cautiously and saw the tuk tuk was gone.

She joined the line of devotees who carried flowers and stick incense into the covered gallery that surrounded the temple complex. She bypassed the well-executed murals that depicted scenes from *The Ramakien*, that Thai epic wherein Prince Rama's wife, Sita, was abducted by the demon king Totsakan.

She looked expectantly for Jeff, but he was nowhere in sight. She remembered the tuk tuk driver's reference to the Emerald Buddha and continued with the crowd toward the entrance of the bot that housed the image.

Removing her sandals, she went inside the bot. Its nave was dark, and it took Jessica a moment to see the Emerald Buddha; a misnomer, really, in that the figure was carved from green jasper. It sat on a tiered pediment amid mosaic umbrellas and miniature silver trees. Below it sat worshipers, many with heads bowed forward to the marble floor.

For Jessica, the smell and smoke of incense made the enclosure claustrophobic. The flames of candles, the only light in the room, flickered wildly, as if on the verge of gutting from lack of oxygen. She tried to find Jeff in the dim light of the room but couldn't. She waited for him to find her, and when that didn't work, she grew nervous.

Reviewing everything that had happened to her, she wondered if she'd somehow missed directions.

Finally, the need for fresh air drove her outside. The cloying smells of cinnamon, flowers, sweat, frankincense and myrhh were like a perfume gone wrong; they dominated everything and made earth-bound thoughts difficult.

Once back outside, she breathed deeply, then relocated her sandals and stepped into them. Crossing the flagstones, she stopped to survey the enclosure. She looked for Jeff but found only strangers, the library, the pantheon, the porcelain *wiharn*, the tall *chedi* bedecked in gold tiles that telegraphed reflected sunlight like a Fourth-of-July sparkler. She shut her eyes to the flickering glare, and when she opened them, she thought she caught a brief glimpse of Jeff on one of the terraces.

She approached the stairs and started up. Halfway, she stopped to get her breath. Her exhaustion seemed so out of character she had to remind herself she'd been in the hospital as early as that morning. She should be back at the Simms's lovely home, lounging in the Simms's lovely garden, and drinking lovely lemonade made by the Simm's lovely servants. But here she was. She was a masochist to comply with Jeff's demand. By rights she should head down the stairs, out the gate, and hail the first cab for four-nine-six Litchi Klong Road. Once back at the house, she could pay the driver with one of the travelers checks secured in a secret pocket of one suitcase. She'd find Nikolas and apologize for needlessly endangering his health in the klong.

Yet, no matter what seemed good in theory she went on up the remaining steps. At the top, she collapsed against the gilded statue of a claw-footed, spritely-tailed, half-woman, half-beast kinnari.

"Hello, Jessica," a very familiar and welcomed voice said from so close it startled her.

7

She turned to see Jeff emerge briefly from the shadow cast by the mythical Himalayan gargoyle, and his outstretched hand took hers to pull her with him into the muggy shade.

"Jeff!" In a fit of spontaneity she threw her arms around him and laid her head against his shoulder. Nestled there, she found that the smell of his familiar cologne reassured her, and so did the fast but steady beat of his heart—or was that merely the echo of her own heartbeat? Only belatedly did she remember that this wasn't the vitriolic greeting she'd planned during her recent journey.

She noticeably trembled when he put his hand in her hair. "I am sorry for the rat race you went through to get here," he told her. "Especially the gun and all. We didn't expect Nikolas to take his job quite so seriously."

His voice grew breathless, and Jessica pulled back far

enough to see his handsome face was unnaturally flushed. Handsomely decked out in what looked to Jessica like Banana-Republic-top-of-the-line, there was an evident stain at one shoulder of his bush jacket.

"You're bleeding!" Realizing that her head-on hello, could hardly have been what the doctor ordered for any wounded man, she tried to escape his arms but he held her close.

"Ever hear of pain made bearable by pleasure?" he asked, smiling down at her.

"Sounds like subject matter for an x-rated movie." Experimentally she rested her fingertips gently atop the telltale spot that formed the stiff stain at his shoulder.

"Nonsense! You'd be doing this injured man a world of good if you'd oblige him with another hug."

"Right!" Jessica agreed facetiously, with no intention of repeating it. "However, maybe we should dispense with further hellos while you explain why you happen to be a wounded man in the first place. Breaking and entering?"

"Is that what Roman's calling it?" Jeff asked, and Jessica saw how he unobtrusively started using his partially unbuttoned jacket as a sling.

"In truth, he's not calling it anything, at least not within my hearing." Jessica decided that wounded or not, Jeff was one of the few men she'd ever seen who was actually handsome with a five-o'clock shadow. Maybe it was the way Jeff's unkempt rugged look seemed to come so perfectly together: stubble; tousled hair that Jessica yearned to comb with her fingers; rumpled jacket without a shirt; the kind of pants with six pockets. All he needed was one of those French Army bush hats, with chin strap and snap-up side to make his ensemble complete.

"What?" she asked, then realized that she'd heard his

question after all. "Roman's pretending nothing happened at all. As far as he's concerned, I'm supposed to think you're off somewhere researching your book. He doesn't know I know that Nikolas showed up at the hospital when everyone thought I was asleep and mentioned that you'd been shot during a break-in."

"Roman lied to you then!"

"Not really. When my sedation wore off, I thought maybe I'd dreamed it, and my doctor agreed so Roman was able to sidestep the issue quite nicely. At the time of your call, I was still under the impression I'd probably dreamed it, although the bug I found in the phone did have me thinking."

He nervously surveyed the surrounding terrain. If someone had been headed up the steps toward them, Jessica thought he would bolt for sure, and she didn't have the energy to run after him.

"How did you find it?" He scanned the area again.

"Your friend told me it was there," Jessica said and didn't want Jeff going anywhere until he gave her some answers. "You know, the one who called me on the pay phone the night of the restaurant bombing, with the mysterious package he wants so badly to sell you. He called me again this morning at the house on the klong. He talked for a couple of minutes, heard some static on the line, and accused me of bugging our conversation. When he hung up, I unscrewed the mouthpiece and found the bug."

Jeff looked noticeably relieved, if not completely convinced.

"Just who is this guy anyway?" Jessica wished she had a handkerchief to wipe some of the sweat from Jeff's suddenly furrowed brow. It struck her that he was possibly running a fever.

"Name of Kenneth Critzer," Jeff said after a brief pause, as if he were debating whether or not to tell her. "He's supposedly some relation, nephew or something, to Jonathan Critzer. Jonathan Critzer was another Yank who, like Powell Whyte, stuck around the Far East after World War II. He drifted into black marketing Far East antiquities and both legal and illegal dealings with Powell. It was Jonathan Critzer who arranged for a lot of the really good artifacts that Powell eventually shipped out of Thailand to the States. I hear Jonathan had no qualms about clandestinely lifting artwork right out of an operational temple if Powell could come up with the right price. And Powell could usually be counted upon to produce the money."

"You 'hear' or you know all that for a fact?" Jessica asked, once again hoping that Jeff wasn't going to blacken Powell Whyte's name with mere hearsay.

"Well, I'd be happy to discuss the rumors with Jonathan Critzer personally," Jeff volunteered magnanimously, "but he was murdered about the same time Powell was. Of course, he wasn't well-known enough to get worldwide obituary notices, like Powell, but you must admit it's curious how the two old cronies bought the farm at about the same time."

"What do the police say?" Jessica intuitively sensed it was all interrelated.

"The police haven't officially closed either murder case," Jeff said, leaning back against the kinnari base.

"And this certain something Kenneth Critzer has to sell you?"

"Powell Whyte's appointment book for the last months of his life," Jeff said. "Kenneth is a little vague about how he happens to have it. He's asking a high enough price for such a seemingly commonplace item, but he knows the record could help me flesh out Powell's last months."

The stain on Jeff's shoulder seemed to be getting bigger. Jessica lifted her hand tentatively toward it and shuddered. "Have you seen a doctor about this?"

"It's a clean wound," he told her, which didn't exactly answer her question. "The bullet went in and out without hitting bone or damaging anything vital. As soon as my body cooperates and replaces the blood I've lost, I'll be in great shape."

"I think you're still bleeding!"

"Some additional bleeding, I'm told, is to be expected." She was reassured. "Maybe if we sat?" Without waiting for her reply he slid down the base of the statue.

"You need a doctor to see to that." Worried, she dropped down beside him. She reached for his free hand, and gave it her best Florence Nightingale squeeze.

"I'll be fine." He squeezed her hand back. "Really."

Shutting her eyes, she leaned back against warm stone. "Whatever am I doing here?" While speaking aloud, the question was aimed more at herself than Jeff.

"I asked you to come, remember?" Jeff answered. He gave her fingers another squeeze. "Maybe the more pertinent question is, 'Why am *I* here?'" Jessica experienced a not-unpleasant shiver and opened her eyes as he continued. "I got away from the museum this morning, and I was boiling mad. I was determined to go public with the story that Roman Whyte was a sneak and a cheat, but I kept hearing your voice inside my head arguing that Roman was an honorable and decent human being. So against all rational and better judgment, I decided to see if he could possibly talk his way out of this one. I'd appreciate hearing your theories on the subject, but my need to prove to you that I could be fair and objective somehow won out over my need for revenge. And over my need to break a story that already seems backed by enough evidence, albeit circumstantial, to indicate Roman is as guilty as sin."

"What evidence?" Jessica thought any evidence Jeff had couldn't possibly be irrefutable if it incriminated Roman. She knew Roman. He was her friend. If he were other than the good guy he seemed, she'd have discovered it long ago.

Then again, someone had bugged her phone.

"Open my jacket pocket," Jeff instructed. "Upper right side."

The pocket flap lifted easily. Jessica reached and found several Polaroid snapshots.

"Bodhisattvas." Two statues had been showcased in close-ups and long shots, leaving no doubt where they'd been photographed. Even Jessica, who'd been at the Powell Whyte Memorial Museum only once, recognized the architecturally distinctive setting. "The statues are phonies," Jeff said. "I only had time to spot these two, but there might be even more."

"How can they be fakes?" Jessica thumbed through the photos again. Several close-ups showed stone faces. Jessica couldn't find the telltale signs of forgery, but she suspected an expert might well be able to do so, just by looking.

"*You* tell *me* how they can be fakes," Jeff challenged.

"Art thieves?" Jessica suggested. "What other logical alternative is there?"

"I don't know if anyone ever explained the security

blanket surrounding that museum to you," Jeff said. "But take it from me, it's all top-of-the-line. I'd like to meet the art thief who could penetrate that system undetected and make off with an artifact."

"*You* penetrated it," Jessica reminded. She already didn't like whatever Jeff was getting at.

"But I came out with only a few photographs and a bullet hole. I didn't piggyback in a couple three-hundred pound fake artifacts, and I didn't piggyback out with any three-hundred pound originals. Besides, unlike your everyday run-of-the-mill art thief, I was invited in."

"Roman invited you?" All kinds of horrible possibilities presented themselves.

"If that were true, I'd be far less willing to give your friend the benefit of a doubt," Jeff said, and Jessica breathed a sigh of relief. "Man by the name of Hua Deng did the honors. He's one of several assigned night duty at the museum."

"Then I assume Hua Deng is responsible for what happened to you," Jessica reasoned. "Not Roman."

"Oh, I don't hold Hua Deng guiltless, not by a long shot," Jeff agreed. "But why would he want me dead? I gave him the money he asked for. He got me in and could have gotten me out just as easily with no one the wiser. So why do you suppose he had someone waiting to blow me away the second I stepped out of the place?"

Jessica didn't need to be a genius to see where this conversation was going. "Roman, on the other hand, does want you dead, is that right?" she asked in disbelief. "Because you're writing a derogatory expose on his uncle? Well, excuse me if I find murder a little excessive."

"Come on, Jessica!" Jeff chided, like a teacher to a schoolgirl who'd entirely missed the point. "We haven't merely been discussing my book, have we?"

"Haven't we?" Jessica suspected that if she weren't getting the point, it was probably because she chose not to.

"Millions of dollars in Thai artifacts," Jeff said, shifting against her. "Hundreds of pieces of Thai master-pieces that Powell Whyte spirited out of Thailand during his lifetime and stockpiled in Los Angeles."

"But these photographs," Jessica said and held up the photos of the bodhisattvas still in her hand, "are of pieces already in Thailand, not in Los Angeles."

"Listen, Jessica. Remember how we once discussed what happens to the whole collection, according to the provisions of Powell's will, if security at the museum were ever to prove inadequate?"

"The collection, and the trust provided to maintain it, goes to Roman," Jessica said, although it was like volunteering a tooth for extraction.

"Right! And what do the fake bodhisattvas in those photos prove, if not that the security at the museum is inadequate? Thereby, Roman has the perfect opportunity to do what?" He didn't wait for her answer but gave her one of his own: "Refuse to ship the remainder of the collec-tion from Los Angeles, that's what! Becoming a few million dollars in artwork richer, right?"

"Your reasoning only goes so far," Jessica objected. "If the bodhisattvas are fake and Roman knows it, why hasn't he gone to the press and claimed government incompetence? If he's as anxious to get his hands on the collection as you say, he would have taken the story to the press before now and claimed the collection by default."

"Maybe he planned for an investigation, resulting from the sudden death of an intruder, to bring the forgeries to light. Maybe I disappointed him by refusing to die on cue."

"But there's been nothing in the news about a break-in, or a shooting, or forgeries found at the museum. Roman wouldn't need your body to start an inquiry, because surely someone heard the shot that wounded you. The gunfire would be reason enough for Roman to question museum security."

"What if he's holding off, just for now, so he can have his cake and eat it, too?" Jeff asked cryptically. Jessica stared at him incredulously. As far as she was concerned, none of his theory was rock solid.

Jeff wasn't through: "What if Roman is keeping quiet for the moment, because he wants it to look as if he's bending over backwards in his cooperation with the Thai government? It would prevent the government from messing around with all the capital he has tied up elsewhere in the Thai economy. His uncle left him the silk company; a lumber company; tin, manganese, and tungsten interests; natural gas leases; and a coconut plantation. To name just a few. If he gives the impression he's unduly anxious to whip the collection out from under the Thai government, the authorities can retaliate by making trouble for his other business interests.

"On the other hand, if he clandestinely arranged for the fakes to replace the originals, then told the government he's prepared to keep the mysterious substitutions a secret so the Thai authorities can find the security breach and plug it, he's the good guy. If he arranged for another breach of museum security by having me sneaked into the museum, then told the government he's willing to overlook that mysterious break-in too while letting the Thai authorities try to make amends, he'll be the good guy yet again.

"One day, though, he'll be able to march up and say, 'Look, you guys, I didn't exert my rights to the collection when several pieces of it were stolen right under your noses. I didn't exert my claim when there was a break-in and the intruder wasn't caught. But since you don't know how the fake bodhisattvas were substituted for the originals, how can you possibly guarantee that the same thieves won't walk away with the rest of it once the rest of the collection is here? Wouldn't it be better if I keep the collection safe in Los Angeles until there's no chance of its dribbling away, piece by piece, here in Thailand?' Who can fault Roman for that concerned reasoning? Then if the Thai government interfered in his interests here, he can scream foul and people will listen.

"You and I both know Powell Whyte did his share to stimulate this country's economy, and many people here see Powell Whyte as their mentor and benefactor. They see his heir, Roman, as Powell Whyte personified. If the Thai government insists their security-lax museum is a better keeper of the art collection than the Whyte family, whom do you think is going to come out on top?"

Jessica gazed over the edge of the terrace. The heat of the day had conjured visible waves that distorted the buildings and gave solid stone the illusion of shimmering movement. Decorative curlicues along the roof eaves seemed to writhe like living snakes.

She mentally reviewed all Jeff said, but it still didn't make sense. "Roman couldn't have done it." Jeff's arm against hers seemed as hard as the stone. "First, he's not the kind of man you're painting him, whether you believe it or not. Second, I don't think it's all that likely he was in a position to arrange for the substitution of fake bodhisattvas for real ones, once the statues were installed in the museum. Or, do you think the Thai government made Roman privy to all the intricate ins and outs of the museum's entire security system?"

"Oh, I think Roman might easily have managed for Hua Deng to allow me in the museum," Jeff objected. "He might have had trouble lugging in the fakes and lugging out the originals, but what if the fakes were substituted in Los Angeles where Roman is in complete charge of security? He could have substituted the fakes at his leisure and shipped them here as the originals. Once the forgeries were on display, he could say, 'I think you have a security breach, because these two bodhisattvas aren't the originals I sent you.'"

"I was at the museum when several of those pieces were uncrated," Jessica said, her defense in high gear. "Dr. Phai Long and Dr. Simtu Rangliti, both of the Thai Institute of Antiquities, were on hand to authenticate them."

"And I think Roman could have had enough cash handy, especially considering the prize, to make doctors Long and Rangliti say black was white. Especially as Dr. Long has an expensive opium habit, and Dr. Rangliti has two mistresses, a wife who lives above her means, and three consumer-oriented kids."

"Can you prove Roman bought off Long and Rangliti?" she demanded.

"I was working on it when somebody took a shot at me," he said, "and I'm still working on it."

"You're telling me you stand ready to go to the world press and convict Roman of complicity on circumstantial evidence!"

"Look, Jessica." For the first time he sounded a little perturbed. "Someone has put me in a position where I don't have many options left, and I figure that someone is Roman. If he's innocent, he'll be able to convince me before I go public with anything. Otherwise, I'll have to take things from there."

"What if Roman doesn't want a meeting?"

"Then I go to the press with what I've got. Maybe I'll even go to the police, although from my past experiences with them I doubt they'd be of much help—except in helping Roman with his cover-up. What I have now can throw Roman in a pretty bad light, and I have no intentions of standing by idly while he takes steps to rectify the job muffed by the gunman who shot me at the museum."

Jessica knew she could bring the two men together, and she had no doubt such a meeting would exonerate Roman. "When would you like to meet with him?" she asked.

"Tomorrow," Jeff suggested.

"This better not mean more dirty taxi floors, suffocating blankets, and detours through dress shops." The very idea made her more tired.

"I'll come to the house where you're staying." Suddenly his voice was lighter, almost carefree. With a surprising grin he checked his watch. "I'll call you tonight at nine sharp to set a time that's convenient all around."

"You think it's safe for you to come to the house?" Jessica asked. She knew she was worrying about two men on opposing sides of the same battle.

"It'll be safe as long as Roman understands that my manuscript, which doesn't currently portray him in a good light, and copies of these photographs will be turned over to the press if I don't check in with someone by a certain time tomorrow night."

"I see." She should have known he was experienced enough in intrigue to keep his bases covered. He didn't need her to worry about him.

"I appreciate your concern, though, Jessica," he said, squeezing her hand. "Really, I do. I know your relationship with Roman is close, and it can't be easy for you to show me any compassion."

She made no effort to pull her hand away. She liked the feel of his curled fingers, and she wanted to pretend for a few moments that they were typical tourists without a care in the world. Instead, she had a final question that needed an answer.

"When I went into that dress shop, I was told to tell the clerk that I came from Mr. Montana."

"The woman doesn't know much English, and we needed something she could easily recognize," Jeff explained.

Which didn't exactly answer her question. "You're Mr. Montana?"

"It's a play on my last name: Billings," he said. "There's a town in Montana called Billings."

Jessica shivered, although she'd told herself she wouldn't.

"Did you know Tim Spencer?" she asked.

"Is this what's called a major shift in conversation?" he queried lightly and gave her fingers a playful squeeze.

"No," she stated firmly, "it isn't. Did you know him?"

"The fellow with U.S. Intelligence who was killed in the bombing at the Normandie? You said he was a Mormon, didn't you?"

"Did you know him?" Jessica repeated.

"No."

"How about Clarence West?"

"Only what I caught about him over the news." He eyed her curiously. "The second 'pig in a poke,' as the terrorist spokesman from the Ron Ron group so pictorially put it. Should I have known him?"

"Tim Spencer and his wife Nora belong to the same branch Roman and I attend when we're in town. The same branch you attended last Sunday. Nora might even have been among those I introduced you to before services."

"And did you introduce me to Tim Spencer?"

"No," Jessica admitted. "He wasn't there."

"Which boils down to what, Jessica?" Jeff's brown eyes looked velvety in the shadow cast by the grotesque kinnari. It seemed totally incongruous to be sitting there, talking about death and destruction.

"I called Nora this morning," Jessica said. "A condolence call. She talked about Tim and how she knew his work was getting to him when he let slip to Clarence West that there was a 'man from Montana' who was a ticking time bomb waiting to go off."

"A man from Montana? You're sure that's what she said?"

"Nora was distraught. Yes, that's what she said."

"It could be sheer coincidence," Jeff said, but he didn't sound convinced.

"I suppose it could," Jessica agreed. The doubt in his voice should have relieved her, but there were so many pieces that still didn't fit.

"What would U.S. Intelligence have to do with me?"

If Jessica had the answer, she wouldn't have asked the question. "I hoped you'd have an idea."

"Well, I frankly haven't a clue," he said, meeting her eyes directly. "But I don't like it."

Neither did she. Letting the possibilities fill her mind,

she didn't like it at all. Jessica thought his handsome face just as handsome in its frown.

"Come on." Jeff struggled to his feet without releasing her hand. "Let's go find you a posh taxi and get you home. It's been another long day."

Jessica reluctantly allowed him to pull her up, then drew him back from the lip of the terrace. "I'm afraid," she told him, wishing she could find any real assurance in his eyes. "Whether you're right or Roman is, one of you is going to get hurt. I don't see any easy resolutions."

"It's too early to worry." He brushed her damp hair off her forehead. "Let's just wait and see how my meeting goes with Roman. If he agrees to see me."

"What if he doesn't? What if the meeting doesn't go well?"

"Let's be optimistic, shall we?"

"It's just that. . . ."

"I know." And somehow she believed he did. Slowly he folded her against him until she could feel her heart beating in time with his. His mouth lowered to hers until their lips met. Tentatively at first, then more firmly. Thought of the future left her mind, leaving only sensations of Jeff, his scent, his texture, the strength of his good arm around her.

"Just in case you're not speaking to me tomorrow at this time," he murmured, breaking the contact of their lips. "I've wanted to kiss you since I first saw you, and the thought that something might happen to keep me from it in the future makes me quite brazen."

His words brought reality back in force. "I really should go." But she knew she wasn't going anywhere until her legs regained their normal strength.

"Feel the sparks?" His head tilted to one side, and his

tongue wet his lips. "I feel the sparks," he told her. "Hot sparks that burn to my core. Seering sparks that brand me a fool for wanting a woman who'll probably fight to the end for the honor of another man."

"Let's be optimistic, shall we?" She echoed his sentiment of a few moments before.

"What is there about you that makes me hope Roman can convince me he's innocent?" Jeff's lemon cologne was more provocative to Jessica than any of the more complex blends the men she associated with always wore.

When his lips touched hers again, a starburst of electricity jolted through Jessica. Automatically, her free hand slid up the back of his neck into his hair. She seemed to melt from the inside out.

The pressure of his mouth took her breath away.

"No," she protested weakly, breaking free. She saw the questioning rich brown pupils of his dilated eyes. "No," she repeated, feeling like a masochist denying herself the pleasure she wanted most.

"Yes," he contradicted. "Yes, yes, oh, yes!"

His good arm pulled her tighter, and his eager mouth sought hers. Jessica ducked away. "This is a complication I don't need."

"Nonsense!" he protested. "Everyone needs a little romance in life."

"Isn't this a little fast?" she asked, freeing herself slowly from his embrace, both relieved and regretful when he let her go.

"Look at all the living you and I have crowded into the few short hours we've known each other," Jeff argued, his voice light even if his words carried all the force and drama of the last two days. "Far more, I'll bet, than you've shared with any other boyfriend."

"Well, I'll give you that," Jessica admitted, giving him a smile to match his own. She was glad to avoid the serious undercurrents that portended a potential emotional disaster.

"It's not as if we have to make a lifetime commitment today," he said. "It merely means we should recognize what's happening and keep our options open."

"Where can we possibly take this to?" Jessica thought their prospects seemed dim indeed.

"Wherever it takes us, I suggest we proceed one step at a time," Jeff ventured.

Jessica sighed and decided her next few steps should take her back to the house. "The sooner you meet with Roman, the sooner he can prove his innocence and the sooner. . . ." She let that daydream taper off to nothing. Her worst fear now was that Roman might not come through for her.

"Come on, and we'll get you a cab," Jeff said, offering his hand.

As they headed down the steps, Jessica told herself she couldn't love a man in so short a time. It had taken her months to make such an important decision in her relationship with Roman. Loving Roman would have been so much easier and uncomplicated than loving Jeff; at least before Jeff cast aspersions on Roman's good character.

Even the very idea that this frustratingly pleasurable pain inside of her could be love was mentally and physically unsettling. It just wouldn't be fair if after all this time of waiting her chance for love came with such impossible odds.

"Some contingencies just can't be planned for, can they?" Jeff asked, as if reading her mind.

If rapport was something Jessica had always

fantasized in an ideal mate, Jeff's insight was all the more disconcerting.

"Then again, what fun would life be if we had a script that spelled out every nuance?"

Jessica wished she could look upon all of this with any sense of *joie de vivre*. But rather than being overjoyed, she was depressed. True love should be exciting and free, not loaded with fear of the future.

"No one said life was easy," Jeff added.

"How's your shoulder?" Jessica said, determined to change the subject.

"Better. There's the proven fact, you know, that love releases a certain something into the system, much the same way chocolate does, that makes a person euphoric."

Jessica wished he'd be a little less anxious to throw the word love around. She might *think* the word, even analyze its meaning and possibilities, but she wasn't ready to state it. Not until she'd more thoroughly sorted things out.

They exited the Wat Phra Keo, and Jessica half expected to find the tuk tuk waiting for them, but there was no sign of it among those lined up to service the steady stream of devotees leaving the Buddhist sanctuary.

Even in the crush, it only took Jeff a few minutes to hail a cab.

Jessica expected Jeff to send her on her way, instead he asked if he could join her. "See how reluctant I am to let you go, even now?" he bantered, scooting in beside her. Immediately, he took her hand and raised her fingers to his lips and kissed them.

"Four-nine-six Litchi Klong Road," Jeff told the driver.

Jessica left her hand in Jeff's, admitting she enjoyed the feel of his fingers intertwined with hers. It gave her comfort and hope for a happy-ever-after ending.

They rode in silence, and she welcomed the respite from talk of love, of Roman, of Thai artifacts, and of gunmen lying in wait. Maybe he, too, knew that silence was often a more valid means of communication than always feeling obligated to fill a void with words.

He settled back in his seat, seemingly satisfied with slowly locking and unlocking his fingers with hers. She settled back and tried to enjoy the simple pleasure of hand holding by watching for street signs: Sanamchi Road, Maharaj Road, Songwat Road, Rama IV Road.

The city continued to reflect its visual overall sense of disordered clutter, but the crowds of people miraculously thinned to virtual non-existence as the taxi turned into the more expensive living area that parenthesized the Litchi Klong.

When the cab was still three blocks away from the entrance to the Simms's compound, on a street deserted except for the line of cars parked along each of its edges, Jeff leaned forward and tapped the driver on the shoulder in signal to stop.

"I'll get out here and find another cab," Jeff said, turning to Jessica. "There's little to be gained if I show up before Roman knows the rules."

"I think you should keep this one," Jessica insisted, because there wasn't another cab in sight. "I'll walk the last couple of blocks."

"Don't you think you've had enough walking for one day?" Jeff asked. "You've been through at least as much as I have these last few hours." But when he didn't immediately hop out, Jessica knew she'd made the right decision.

"Even so, I don't have a bullet hole in my shoulder.

And I expect you to go get some proper attention for that wound immediately." She tried to exit on such a good line, but he continued to hold her hand captive.

"This really is a marvelous thing that's happening between us, Jessica." He kissed her hand again. There was something about the way his warm breath brushed her fingertips that gave her pleasurable goose bumps.

"I'll be expecting your call at nine," Jessica said, not voicing her agreement that they were talking "marvelous" here. So what if she felt somehow deprived of a vital part of herself when he finally turned her hand free?

Once on the curb she watched the taxi pull away and turn the corner. The way the sun reflected off the car windows, she couldn't see Jeff inside, but she knew he could see her, and she wondered what he was thinking.

More to the point, what was she thinking? As she walked slowly down the road toward the Simms's compound, she wished she could put her jumbled thoughts and emotions into crystal-clear perspective. Her mind was in total disarray.

Vaguely, she noticed a blue van parked in the way to the house. When its side panel slid open, she heard the squeal of metal against metal, the same sound which had accompanied the opening of the warehouse door when she'd changed taxis en route to meet Jeff.

A horrid dampness suddenly locked itself securely over her mouth and nose, the eye-watering stench of it burning her throat and nose.

"Jeff!" Desperately she called for the one man who had become such an important part of her life. For her effort, she received another debilitating intake of noxious fumes. She struggled against them and against her assailant, but her sense of reality paled.

She managed to free one hand and fought against the mask covering her face. But she couldn't muster the strength to continue.

She was losing consciousness, and she knew it. Her legs buckled, and she waited for the jarring impact of her knees against the pavement. Instead, she felt a brief sensation of floating, followed by an inky oblivion.

8

Nausea gripped her. Her head throbbed. She tried to feel her forehead for any trace of a fever. She couldn't move either hand.

"You're handcuffed to the door of the van." Jessica identified the voice immediately. When she opened her eyes, however, she didn't recognize the man seated cross-legged on the mattress that covered the floor.

Jessica decided he was probably in his late sixties. His white hair was a thinning fringe around a bald pate. His face was all sharp angles and points, his cheeks hollow. His prominent Adam's apple was part of a skinny neck that was encircled, but not touched, by the buttoned collar of his shirt. His tie, a nondescript strip of muted russet, was open along its knot so both ends trailed below the waistband of his jeans.

"Mr. Kenneth Critzer, I presume?" It was difficult to

be Henry Stanley clever when her mouth would hardly move.

"Ah, you've done your homework!" The man leaned back against the door on his side of the van.

There were curtains on the windows, but the light getting through told Jessica it was still day. She just didn't know which day.

"How long have I been out?" She licked lips dry enough to crack.

"Mere minutes."

She tried to find a more comfortable position, glad the soiled mattress was softer than the taxi floors she was used to.

"I am sorry for the crude way you were abducted," he apologized, "but you rather caught my men off guard, coming at them as you did from an entirely different direction than I'd led them to expect. It forced them into a bit of spur-of-the-moment improvisation. I'd told them you were only recently out of the hospital and probably wouldn't be up and around until sometime tomorrow, at the earliest. Luckily, I'd left them this." He held up a photograph of Jessica and Jeff at the door of the Spicy Whiskey.

"You took that picture?" Jessica tried to remember anyone on the street with a camera Sunday who'd looked like Kenneth Critzer.

"One of my men took it. I've been somewhat indisposed myself."

Jessica agreed he didn't look well.

"Something is going around that could be the death of me, you might say. So, I'm desperate for more amiable climes. Which brings me to you."

"And, I suppose, to Powell Whyte's appointment book?"

"Billings told you, did he?" Kenneth didn't sound surprised.

"Are these handcuffs really necessary?" No matter how hard she tried, she couldn't get comfortable.

"Do try to endure the minor inconvenience for a few minutes more," Kenneth insisted. "This shouldn't take long."

"I find it all overly dramatic, no matter what the length," Jessica sighed. "Wouldn't it be easier to pick up the phone and give Jeff a call? From what he's told me, he'll be more than pleased to get together with you to buy what you're offering."

"Disappointingly, Billings managed to lose the man I had tailing him," Kenneth bemoaned. "So, I'm not just too sure where he can be reached these days. Do you have any ideas?"

"No." The only thing she knew was when he'd be calling Roman.

"Speaking of telephone calls, let me apologize for the way I ended ours. I've grown admittedly more paranoid than usual these days—what with my health problem—and I'm afraid I wrongly assumed you bugged your phone. Oh, I don't doubt the phone was bugged," he added quickly, "because I've become quite expert in detecting that sort of thing. On the other hand, I wasn't aware at the time that four-nine-six Litchi Klong Road was the residence of Mr. and Mrs. Cecil Simms. Once I made that connection, your innocence was apparent."

"Oh?" Jessica didn't get the connection.

"Most businessmen with residences in Thailand have all their incoming and outgoing calls automatically recorded for later replay nowadays," Kenneth explained. "It's *de rigueur* as a way of quickly monitoring crank calls, ransom demands, death threats, and whatever else happens to come over the phone lines. Terrorists are such volatile people. I wouldn't recommend involvement with them at any level." He smiled, and it did nothing whatsoever to improve his looks. "They can be dangerous to your health, if you get my drift."

"You mean Cecil Simms bugs his own phones?" Jessica asked. It meant Roman couldn't have been responsible and made Jeff's claims more impossible.

"All quite logical, once you realize how much Mr. Simms is worth worldwide," Kenneth told her. "I, on the other hand, have come upon hard times, due to the recent failure of a business deal. It's very important to my well-being that I receive the money Billings is offering for Powell Whyte's appointment book. Quite aside from the dangers to me from certain unsatisfied customers of my soured business deal, I'm additionally skittish because Whyte and my uncle were both murdered. For all I know, the killer may still be around. And if word is out that the book has surfaced, I may be next on the list."

"Why would anyone kill for an appointment book?" The metal cuffs chafed her wrists, but trying for a more comfortable position seemed futile.

"Why indeed?" Kenneth asked with a shrug. "Admittedly, I can find nothing within its pages that would seem the motive for two murders, but if it's as innocuous as it seems, why did my uncle give it to me for safekeeping? It's only because I thought it might be more than it seemed that I've held on to it for so long. Now, however, my precarious financial predicament dictates that I delegate the solving of the riddle to Billings and pass the risk on to him."

Jessica's left leg was falling asleep. She tightened her

leg muscles, then relaxed them to stimulate circulation.

"What might seem a simple exchange of cash for mer-
chandise to you and Billings has become an exercise for me
in covering my back." Kenneth seemed totally unaware of
her growing discomfort, and Jessica fought to keep her
mind focused on the discussion. "Billings won't try
anything funny with an innocent like you as courier."

"Why would he try anything funny, anyway, when
he's so obviously interested?"

"I do believe he finds the asking price a bit
exorbitant."

"Well, maybe he does." She didn't think she'd been
yanked off the street a second time that day just to play
middleman.

"I don't plan to let him attempt a renegotiation of
price at the last minute," Kenneth said. "If anything, I
should be upping the ante to compensate me for all I've
done recently to assure his continued good health. You do
know, of course, to what I'm referring."

"I haven't a clue."

Kenneth smiled sadly, and it was no more flattering to
him than his last smile. Jessica wondered if anything would
make him more attractive.

"What are you trying to tell me?" she asked. "Things
will move along far more quickly if we stop playing twenty
questions."

"I really thought Inspector Chuab would have given
you the good news by now," Kenneth complained. "Oh,
not its connection to me, since he doesn't have that, but
enough for you to put two and two together. It's already
made the news, you know."

"I've been out this afternoon, remember?" Jessica
wished he'd get to the point. She also wished they'd get to

their destination soon. She was tired and miserable and quickly becoming impatient. "I haven't seen a newspaper or heard a radio."

"Yes, that might explain it."

"Explain what?"

"Because of me, Inspector Chuab has apprehended those responsible for shooting at you and Billings on the Chao Phraya River."

"Because of you?"

"The man I had follow Billings, the man who took this photograph—" He again lifted the picture of Jeff and Jessica at the entrance to the Spicy Whiskey. "At the time of the shooting he was in position to take a few additional pictures of a Mr. Naikor Pisanul, who is employed at one of the local shipping depots for Whyte Silk Consortium. His son also works for Whyte in some other menial capacity. Granddad was with Powell when the business was first started. Thus we have three generations of Pisanuls who worked for the Whytes and were happy to do so. Well, Grandfather Pisanul might be dead, but the other two decided to scare Billings away from doing the hatchet job he was out to do on the memory of Powell Whyte. Unfortunately for the Pisanuls and their accomplices, the sniper was photographed while they left the scene of the crime. Now Billings won't be bothered any further from that particular quarter. So you see, my asking price for the appointment book only seems exorbitant when the hidden extras aren't included in the package."

"Of course, if someone killed Jeff, you'd be left without any buyer, wouldn't you?" Jessica didn't buy his Good-Samaritan routine for a moment. The man was a self-serving sleaze, and Jeff should watch his back when dealing with Mr. Critzer. "And without a buyer, your health might deteriorate at even a faster rate than anticipated, because there'd be no money for a cure."

"So, don't thank me," Kenneth said with a ludicrous pout. "Do, however, please see that you and the money are at the Saladang Intersection, at the southwest corner of Lumpini Park, Wednesday at one o'clock sharp. Tell Billings I expect you to be there alone, or the exchange will be aborted."

"And, if I can't reach Jeff?"

"Maybe you'll come up with the money for him," Kenneth suggested. "I'm sure he'll pay you back. Quite frankly, I've reached a point where I have to decide whether my chances for survival are better served in Bangkok, waiting for the possibility of money, or away from Bangkok, without a *baht* to my name. If you knew the people out to get me, you might think I've already overstayed my time in this city. So if you're not there, Billings won't hear from me again any time soon. In the interim, give him this." He took a folded piece of paper from his shirt pocket and stuffed it in the pocket of Jessica's blouse. Jessica cringed, even though he didn't touch her. "I apologize, again, for the extent my men mussed you up. I instructed them not to mistreat you, but you do look as if you'd been drug through the mud."

"What's on the paper?" Jessica asked, trying not to think about all she'd been through that day.

"It's a page from Powell Whyte's appointment book," Kenneth said. "Now, if you'll excuse me." He shifted his position and opened the rear door.

As soon as he exited and closed the door behind him, the van began to move again. Jessica hoped she was about to be released, but she wasn't encouraged by the cuffs that still chafed her wrists.

About fifteen minutes later the van stopped. Wearily she waited for what would happen next.

The door slid open to admit someone even uglier than Kenneth Critzer, someone who had kinky blond hair, a large and flattened nose, jowly cheeks, pinprick eyes, and who wore only a pair of dirty coveralls. He smelled of sweat and onions, his voice so guttural Jessica could hardly interpret his: "Don't make noise!"

Struggling against a fresh wave of fear, she stiffened, finding little comfort in the keys he carried. Roughly he unlocked her handcuffs. "Get out!" He left as abruptly as he'd arrived, and Jessica heard the front door of the van shut while she was still willing her cramped limbs to function. Her feet barely hit the pavement when the van barreled away, leaving her weaving on the exact spot where she'd been picked up.

Tentatively, she took a first step toward the Simms's compound which was only a couple of blocks away but seemed like miles. She took a few more steps to assure herself of her balance and hurried toward the safety of the house.

Nikolas waited just inside the front gate, and his presence welcomed her. He might have been the pursuer earlier, now he seemed like safe haven. He assumed an immediate on-guard martial-arts stance but only for a moment. "Roman is in the house," he said. "Can you make it on your own?"

Jessica knew she must look terrible, but considering everything, she had arrived in far better shape than she might have.

"I'm okay," Jessica assured him. "Are you?"

"Me?" He sounded genuinely surprised.

"Your dip in the klong," she reminded.

"Oh," he said. "I've been worse."

"Yes." Jessica shivered. Undoubtedly there were prescription drugs to take care of such things. Maybe massive doses of antibiotics to kill the germs before they got started with their nastiness. She only hoped she never had to find out.

Entering the house, her footsteps brought Roman hurrying to meet her. "Jessica?" He'd changed clothes since last she'd seen him: from ivory-white silk suit to black silk tuxedo. His cologne smelled of musk, oak, leather and smoke. "Are you okay?" he asked, sounding genuinely concerned.

"I'm fine."

"Sure?" He took both her hands, and the play of expression on his face as he looked at her showed the effects of the day better than a mirror.

"Nothing a bit of rest won't cure."

"You've seen Billings, haven't you?" he said. "And he's told you about the break-in?"

"He said he was invited in by someone called Hua Deng," Jessica told him, aware of a defensive note in her voice. "He thinks you're involved in an attempt to reclaim your uncle's art collection under the terms of default in the will. He thinks you replaced a couple artwork originals with forgeries, and he thinks you had him shot at the museum. He believes it's a plot to prove the Thai government is incapable of providing the kind of security the provisions of your uncle's will demand." The recitation of Jeff's allegations made her feel still more miserable. How could she believe Roman fit the picture Jeff painted of him? As much as she cared about Jeff, and, yes, she could finally confess she did care about him, she couldn't agree that Roman was a scoundrel. "He's planning to go to the press with the story," Jessica concluded, "although he wants to meet with you first, to listen to your version. He's calling here tonight at nine to hear if you'll agree to a meeting."

"You say the man who gave him access to the museum was Hua Deng?" Roman asked. Jessica would have preferred answers, rather than more questions. She wanted him to convince her that she hadn't misplaced her faith in him over the years.

"He's on the night staff," Jessica said.

Roman reached for the phone and dialed. "Whyte here," he said shortly. "I have Jessica Miller with me. . . Yes, she's seen him, and Billings has concocted a story that I've replaced originals with forgeries and plan to reclaim my uncle's art collection by blaming a faulty security system. Luckily, he's giving us a chance to salvage by calling in tonight at nine to set up a meeting to hear my side. . . . I don't think we have any other choices, do you? What's more, may I remind you that I've said from the moment of Jessica's involvement with the man that she should be put abreast of the situation?" He smiled at Jessica, and she hoped that the explanations would finally clarify the murky waters. "Yes, I'll wait for you to get back to me," Roman continued into the phone, "but you can tell your superiors I'm going to tell her, with or without their okay." He checked his watch and listened a few seconds more. "Yes, I can give you that long, but it wouldn't be safe to wait longer than that. By the way, I think I may have identified one of the Ron Ron 'moles' at the museum. Someone named Hua Deng invited Billings onto the premises."

Jessica couldn't imagine what the Ron Ron had to do with any of this.

Roman hung up and turned back to Jessica.

"Tell me there are answers to all of this that will allow me to keep you as a friend and keep Jeff as a. . . ." She didn't finish, instead she walked over to him and stepped into his opened arms. She rested her cheek against his chest while he gave her a reassuring hug. She was convinced these weren't the arms of a blackguard. Nor was this heart, beating loudly in her ear, that of a conniver out to wrest a fortune in artwork from the Thai government.

"Yes, there are those kinds of answers," Roman assured her, and she believed him. "And, if I'd had my way, you *and Jeff* would have had your answers before things got to this state of affairs." Roman's breath stirred her hair, his cologne a heady aroma as complicated as the web in which they were emeshed. "Unfortunately, my hands have been tied."

"Tied by whom?" Jessica marveled how the embraces of the different men in her life could be mutually reassuring but exist on entirely different emotional plains. She felt safe within Roman's arms. She felt comforted by his touch and by the beat of his heart in his chest. He instilled all of that in her, but in Jeff's arms she experienced all of that and more.

He held her slightly away from him. "I need a little more time, though," he said, and Jessica's heart hurt. She wanted her answers now, on the spot, spontaneous, untainted by deliberation that might produce lies. "Not an inordinate amount of time, mind you," Roman said, as if he'd read her mind. "Just enough for someone to get back to me on the phone. Less time, possibly, than it takes for you to freshen up a bit. You do look as if you've had a hard day."

"Thanks," she said wearily. What else could she do?

Scream? Shout? She wondered why Roman Whyte had to check with *anyone* before he took action.

"I promise I'll tell you everything, whether I get authorization or not," Roman assured her. "I would, however, like to give them a chance to make it official."

"I could use a bath," Jessica confessed, prepared to give him the time he requested. Not enough time, though, to take a leisurely tub bath. She knew if she succumbed to hot, steamy water and luxurious lavender-scented bubbles, she might never get out. Luckily, she knew the modern conveniences of the Simms's bathroom could offer her a quick shower.

"After your bath, maybe you could use a little something to eat," Roman suggested.

"I really don't feel all that hungry." Actually, she was convinced the secret to successful dieting was a regimen of being shot at, being almost blown up by terrorists, and being kidnapped. The *To Die or Diet Book*. It sounded like something Jessica could write in her sleep. She wondered if Jeff could interest his publisher friends in letting her give it a try.

"I'll have the cook make chicken sandwiches," Roman insisted.

"Somehow you don't look dressed for Colonel Sanders." Jessica ran her fingers down the edge of one Brussels-antique-lace panel that fronted his dress shirt.

"Actually, I find myself even less up to the meal I'd originally planned for this evening than you are," Roman admitted. "Can I have a rain check on that one?"

"That depends upon what you have to tell me after my shower," Jessica said noncommittally. She wanted to believe he'd have all the right answers in so short a time.

Her shower convincingly argued its benefits over those of bathing in a tub. It subjected Jessica's battle-weary body to several sources of water that bombarded her from every conceivable angle. By minuscule adjustments of a master control, Jessica graduated spray from mist to gale-force intensity, from steady stream to pulsating surges. The latter pounded against her soreness in a masseur-like massage that teetered her precariously on the razor's edge between sheer bliss and sheer agony.

The panacea of her man-made cocoon seduced her into lingering far longer than she intended. Every time her mind told her to reach out and interrupt the flow, her body refused. She wanted to stay where she was, wallowing in a sense of well-being. The water splashed her body, molding her in a liquid armor that shielded her from the emotional slings and arrows of the outside world.

"Don't fool yourself!" She mined the depths of her self-control and turned off the water. "You're not immune to anything, and you haven't gotten where you are today by sticking your head in the sand." No matter how this turned out, she knew it was best to face reality head-on, the way she'd met most major crises in her life. She'd identify the problem, confront it, determine the required solution, and get on with her life.

Despite her resolve, she trembled as she doned red-embroidered, white terry-cloth caftan and turban. She didn't want to lose Roman as a friend. She didn't want to lose Jeff and all the possibilities of that barely-explored relationship.

Roman waited in the small, intimate room just off the library. He was hanging up the phone when she entered.

"Sit down and have a sandwich." He crossed the room to take her hand and lead her toward a chair. The coffee table was loaded with a platter of chicken sandwiches, bottled water, and fruit.

"Does that mean bad news?" she asked. The sight of all that food created a sudden appetite, and she wondered how many hours it had been since she'd last eaten.

"It means a bit of food is in order, whether we think we're hungry or not." Roman sat on the sofa across from her.

Jessica wondered if he were stalling. There were enough sandwiches to keep them occupied for hours. Nevertheless, she gave him the benefit of the doubt and helped herself.

While they ate Roman began his explanations.

"Ten years ago, there was a major drug bust in Miami Beach," Roman said.

Jessica wondered what drugs in Florida had to do with all the recent events in Thailand, but she didn't ask. Surely he'd get to that if she waited long enough.

"The bust took place on the private estate of a man called Quinland Maxwell, who'd been trafficking in narcotics even before it became so fashionable with organized crime. Drug dealing, in fact, had made Mr. Maxwell a very rich man, and it had allowed him to indulge in his penchant for acquiring Incan artifacts. In the raid his collection was seized along with all the rest of his property. In time U.S. government experts appraised the collection for sale at public auction. Among the pieces were several pots thought to be copies of originals in the Corro de Paseo Museum de Nationale in Bogota, Colombia. They were such good copies, however, that one of the experts checked farther, and to everyone's surprise, he began insisting that the museum had the copies, and Maxwell's collection contained the originals.

"Six years ago, Texas millionnaire, Thomas Gordon-Mills died. In a basement vault of his Dallas home were supposed copies of the silver Viking scabbard clip and the silver cloak fastener on display in a small museum outside Malmo, Sweden. Only the copies weren't copies, and the originals weren't originals.

"Three years ago, a bronze lion was offered to the Getty Museum by an anonymous Italian seller as the companion piece to the 'Lion by Milo,' on exhibit at the Museum Herculaneum, south of Naples. Getty bought the bronze, although the Italian government has since begun international legal proceedings, insisting the Getty lion is the original which was stolen from the Museum Herculaneum and that a clever substitution had been left by the thieves at the Museum.

"Two years ago. . ." He paused meaningfully. "Suffice it to say there are other documented examples of originals that have turned up where they shouldn't, and fakes that have done the same."

Jessica hadn't yet made whatever the connection Roman was aiming for. With his eyes, though, he begged her just to give it time. "Ten years ago the terrorist group Julio Azul operated in Colombia and claimed responsibility for the car bomb that went off outside the U.S. Embassy in Bogota and killed three people.

"Six years ago the terrorist group Sven Nacht operated in Sweden and claimed responsibility for the kidnapping and brutal murder of U.S. businessman Gayland Clark.

"Three years ago the terrorist group Ciao Bianco operated in Italy and claimed responsibility for the assassination of U.S. Vice Consul Henry Jacoinson.

"Evidence now indicates that the activities of all three terrorist groups were financed by the stealing of antiquities and selling both the originals and forgeries on the black market. Other information demonstrates that terrorist groups in France, Spain, Turkey, Greece, Lebanon, and Nicaragua, to name just a few, have done the same thing."

"And you think some terrorist group is doing the same thing here?" Jessica asked noncommittally.

"Two years ago," Roman continued, "there was a secret symposium on terrorism under the sponsorship of Fidel Castro in Sangua la Grande, Cuba. As part of those ten days of sessions, one of the topics of discussion concerned the black marketing of stolen original artwork and the black marketing of forgeries of original artwork as a valid means of financing revolution. Han Anyank, the prime mover behind the Ron Ron here in Thailand, was there. He heard how Third World countries are, on the whole, ill equipped to come up with sufficient capital to safeguard their archaeological heritage from determined and well-organized art thieves."

"The Powell Whyte Memorial Museum didn't have to rely on a monetarily-strapped government to finance its security system," Jessica reminded him. "Your uncle saw to that in his will."

"Even the best security systems, though, can't be expected to stand up to machinations launched from within," Roman insisted. "Which was another point emphasized at the meeting in Cuba.

"A year ago the small museum at Roi Et, just north of here, was destroyed by a mysterious explosion and fire. Less than a month later, Thai artifacts, originally reported destroyed in that explosion, were offered for sale on the black market.

"Eight months ago, a figure of Uma, Khmer-style, which had been stolen from the permanent Thai collection at the Antiquities Museum in Rat Buri, was believed clandestinely sold to a private buyer in Bern, Switzerland, for an estimated sixty thousand U.S. dollars. It's now believed some of that money financed both the recent bombing of the Northwest Orient reservation office at the Siam Center and the bombing of the Normandie Room restaurant."

"And the forgeries at the Powell Whyte Memorial Museum?" Jessica asked.

"U.S. Intelligence anticipated my uncle's collection would appear to be a particularly juicy plum for the Ron Ron's plucking," Roman said. "Every piece is superior-grade, worth astronomical amounts to private dealers who couldn't hope to pick up anything comparable via legal channels. The plan was to monitor the collection during its transfer and installation and entrap the Ron Ron in the act of stealing and/or replacing one of the pieces. The ultimate result, it was hoped, would be the eradication of the scum-ball organization. With that objective, U.S. Intelligence approached me and the Thai government for our mutual assistance and cooperation."

"Which you both gave."

"Which we both gave."

"However, there were snags." The pieces were starting to fall into place.

"Aren't there always snags?" Roman said with opened palms. "In this case, despite all the monitoring by U.S. Intelligence, the Thai government, myself, the Ron Ron somehow replaced and walked off with two artifacts before detection. Oh, it was obvious it had to be an inside job, but no one had a clue until you told me Hua Deng had arranged for Jeff to obtain entrance to the museum. I'd say Hua Deng identified himself as one of the Ron Ron by extending Jeff that invitation."

"You believe the Ron Ron has so many moles inside that despite all your precautions they could switch the two artifacts without your knowledge? And that you, U.S. Intelligence, and the Thai government didn't have a clue?" she asked incredulously.

"The Ron Ron has a lot of ways to entice men to silence and cooperation," Roman argued. "Elimination. The death of a loved one or loved ones. Horrible torture. Mutilation."

"Giving you that, why would the Ron Ron go to the bother of setting Jeff up for a murder?" Jessica asked. "Which is what you're insinuating Hua Deng did."

"Jeff made waves whenever he raised the possibility of fakes in the museum," Roman reminded her. "Certainly the Ron Ron didn't want Jeff out there pointing an accusing finger, even if his finger was pointed at me."

"They thought that noisily killing Jeff on the museum steps wasn't going to have people asking questions?"

"Whatever the questions resulting from Jeff's untimely demise, they could be answered by labeling him a common thief, killed in the act. Jeff would have been killed inside the museum. It would be easy enough to imply he'd been in before, in order to exchange original artifacts for forgeries. With that explanation the Ron Ron would have eliminated him and the threat of exposure. They would also have provided themselves with a scapegoat on whom to blame the thefts already committed — *if* the thefts were uncovered during any investigation of Jeff's murder.

"More likely, though, the Ron Ron hoped Jeff's death would be explained as the accidental result of a nosy reporter, caught somewhere that he shouldn't have been. That would cast no doubts on the validity of any piece of the collection. That course seems even more likely, since we'd planned to give the Ron Ron every chance to become overconfident. We'd arranged for the appointments of Dr. Long and Dr. Rangliti as Thai art experts on the museum staff. Dr. Long has an expensive opium habit, and Dr. Rangliti is a ladies' man with a wife who'd rather have another cold piece of jewelry to keep her company on hot nights than her husband. Their habits made both men vulnerable to a Ron Ron approach. We could probably march Dr. Long and Dr. Rangliti through the museum at this very moment, and they'd swear the two fakes are real. Our ability to recognize the fakes from the originals depended upon my familiarizing myself with the originals while they were still in L.A."

"Why did you keep the shooting at the museum quiet once you heard it had occurred?"

"We didn't want to draw any attention to the museum that might compromise our operation," Roman said. "A public investigation of the shooting might have turned up the fakes, and/or caused questions to be asked that might have proved embarrassing to the Thai government, which was officially in charge of museum security. I might then have been asked whether I considered it grounds for claiming the collection for myself. All unwanted publicity. In the end, we decided it would be best to try and find Jeff before he did anything more to gum up the works. We knew it was Jeff at the museum that night from a tape made by a security camera."

"And you don't want the collection for yourself?" Jessica asked, only because she knew Jeff would ask it.

"If my uncle stole all or part of the collection from the Thai people, he was prepared to make amends, albeit posthumously. Who am I to deny him his penance, as late as it may have been in coming? Besides, I already have more than enough money to last one man a lifetime."

It was the first time Jessica had heard Roman admit even the possibility that his uncle might have acquired the artifacts by other than honest methods.

"Tell me how it is that only you and Jeff were able to walk down those rows of statues at the museum and pinpoint the fakes?" Jessica felt driven to continue her role of devil's advocate.

"I spotted them because I was being counted upon to find them if an exchange were made," Roman said. "Jeff found them because he wanted to find them for a story. Do you know how many forgeries pass the inspection of supposed experts in reputable museums every year? There's a kouros at the Getty Museum that some experts say is sixth-century B.C., others swear it's twentieth-century A.D. There's a sarcophagus at the Boston Museum of Fine Arts that could be 450 B.C. or 1900 A.D., depending upon which expert is asked. There are yeas and nays for Raphael's *La Fornarina* at the Barbierini Gallery in Rome, as well as for the bust of Caracalla in the Kansas City Nelson-Atkins Museum. And you wonder why the Ron Ron can be confident their forgeries will go undetected here in Thailand? If the experts can't always tell a bodhisattva, pre-Ankor style, from a bodhisattva, Khmer style, do you expect doubts of any kind to be voiced by the ordinary man in off the street?"

"Tell me about Tim Spencer and Clarence West," Jessica said. "They were working with you on this?"

"Yes," Roman admitted. "Assigned to the project by U.S. Intelligence."

"Killed because they were on the project?"

"Killed because such men are always marked for

murder by the terrorist element," Roman offered an alternative. "Despite our early fears that their involvement in the project might have been an additional reason for their assassination by the Ron Ron, we determined that wasn't the case. The final verdict was that they were killed because they were U.S. Intelligence, not because of the specific assignment they were involved in at the time."

Jessica helped herself to another half a sandwich. With her apprehension relieved, she realized she was ravenously hungry after all.

9

Roman was gone by the time Jeff called.

"Tomorrow morning at ten," he told Jessica. She would have liked to talk longer, but Jeff seemed cautious and as anxious as Jessica was for Jeff to hear what Roman had said, she preferred to let Roman tell him. Jessica found Roman's explanation feasible, but she remained admittedly biased on his behalf. Jeff might find holes and implausibilities that Jessica couldn't see, let alone explain away.

The next morning Jessica was downstairs by the time Roman and his support group arrived. To her delight one of them returned her purse which had finally been recovered from the runaway dugout on the Chao Phraya River. Jessica checked the contents and found nothing missing, not even her money.

She took her purse to her bedroom and laid its

contents on the dresser for airing, then threw the smelly thing away.

Roman and his companions enjoyed a breakfast prepared by the cook. Jessica, though, was too nervous to eat.

She positioned herself in a teak chair adjacent to the front door. When the knocker sounded a few minutes before ten, she answered it before the houseboy could put in a token appearance.

"Hi," Jeff said. His arm rested in a professional-looking sling, but it didn't prevent him from leaning forward to exchange a quick kiss of welcome with her. He wore a pewter-colored safari shirt of Egyptian cotton, its epaulets complementing the distinctive military cut of his Australian army pants with Dutch-inspired ankle tabs. His French Legion boots were of gray cotton canvas. Jessica had to admit he looked good, complete with his fresh shave and citrusy cologne.

"How's the shoulder?" she asked, standing back to let him in.

"Actually, it's coming along quite nicely." But she could tell his mind wasn't centered on their interchange. He seemed to sniff the air, much like a deer who senses a predator in the bushes.

"Roman isn't alone," she said. "He brought along a couple of people he feels can give you a better perspective than he can."

"He thinks he can convince me, then?" Jeff didn't sound surprised. "You have to give the guy credit for moxie."

"They're in the garden." Jessica turned to lead the way, but Jeff reached out to stop her.

As always, she marveled at how his touch could set

her aglow. More than anything, she desperately wanted Jeff to be as convinced as she about Roman's innocence.

"You've heard what he has to say?" Jeff asked, less a question than a statement.

Jessica nodded and couldn't resist an impulse to touch him. She ran her fingers gently down his arm to the large fingers still curled around her forearm. Fine black hair grew across the back of his hand.

"Okay, then." He turned his hand to catch her lingering fingers and delivered a reassuring squeeze.

The table had been cleared of everything but a bowl of fresh fruit, and all three men stood in unison when Jessica and Jeff entered the garden. With his hand on her waist, Jeff led her toward the comfortable grouping of lawn furniture.

"Jeff Billings." Roman introduced him to the group, then turned to the man at his left. "You know Inspector Chuab, Jeff."

"Yes." Jeff returned the inspector's nod.

· "I don't believe you know Conrad Tiller, senior U.S. Intelligence officer at the U.S. Embassy here in Bangkok," Roman continued.

"Mr. Billings," Conrad motioned Jeff into one of the chairs. If Jeff was surprised by the presence of a top U.S. Intelligence agent, Jessica thought he hid it nicely.

They all sat down.

"Jessica tells us you have a story prepared for the press," Conrad said, and it was obvious to Jessica he was the one who'd lead the conversation from there. He didn't press for Jeff's confirmation about the news story, probably because he considered any such verification superfluous.

"I'm here to listen," Jeff said, sounding totally

objective.

Jessica's stomach spasmed nervously. She hoped that whatever Conrad said would be consistent with Roman's story. She didn't want deviations now that she'd been given hope that her faith in both Jeff and Roman hadn't been unwarranted.

"There was a major drug bust in Miami Beach ten years ago. . ." Conrad began.

"So, there you have it," Conrad concluded, and Jessica breathed easier. Not only hadn't the explanation by Conrad differed from what Roman had told her the afternoon before, but it seemed even more plausible this second time around. However, she knew what she thought didn't really count, not in the long or short run. It was Jeff's analysis that mattered.

Jeff met Jessica's eyes and arched an eyebrow as if to ask, "I'm supposed to believe this?" Or it might have illustrated his genuine surprise in having heard a better explanation of events than his own. Weighing the alternatives, Jeff turned back to Conrad. "And if I accept all of this, what else do you want from me?"

Jessica could hardly control the welling of emotion inside her. If Jeff believed Conrad and Roman, well. . .

Suddenly, she wanted to be alone with Jeff. She wanted to lose herself in his arms and discuss what it all meant to the two of them. Unfortunately there was more involved here than their newly-found love.

"We want time," Conrad said. "Time to press Mr. Hua Deng for some answers that might lead to the Ron Ron. Time to make all the efforts we've already expended on this project pay off for us."

"You really think you can get anything out of Hua

Deng?" Jeff asked. "How do you know he hasn't already disappeared?"

"We picked him up last night," Inspector Chuab said.

"But you said the Ron Ron would have bought his silence with threats."

"We have our own means of persuasion," the inspector replied.

"How much time are we talking here?" Jeff asked.

"A week," Conrad estimated. "Give or take a couple of days."

"All right, I'll give you a week, give or take a couple of days," Jeff conceded, and Jessica wanted to pinch herself to assure she wasn't dreaming. "After which, I reserve the right to reconsider my position," Jeff qualified.

"Fair enough." Conrad clapped his open hands on his knees.

"I only wish you'd briefed me on all of this a lot sooner."

"We apologize for that," Conrad told him. "In military jargon, it's called need-to-know and for you, it was a little late in coming. Tim Spencer suggested bringing you in as soon as he realized your intentions. He referred to you as a ticking time bomb just waiting to go off and cause all kinds of trouble. However, too many of my superiors believed the fewer people in on this the better it would be. Those same people argued against telling Miss Miller anything, even though Roman kept insisting she needed to know. I expect you'd both still be in the dark if you hadn't found a way to lodge a burr beneath a couple of behinds."

"Before I excuse myself to check on the interrogation of Mr. Hua Deng," Inspector Chuab said, standing to button his coat, "I'd like to hear just how it was that Mr.

Billings came to suspect there were forgeries in the collection in the first place."

"Just a little hint dropped by someone who works at the museum," Jeff admitted.

"Loose lips sink ships," Conrad said. "It might be best if we checked out your source, Billings. What do you say?"

"One of the janitors," Jeff conceded. "A Cambodian refugee named Khon Ubon. He told me he knew a fake bodhisattva, pre-Ankor style, when he saw one. His uncle was an antique dealer before displacement during the war."

"A janitor!" Conrad came to his feet with a shake of his head. "To think some janitor was responsible for almost spoiling it all!"

The discussion ended quickly after that, and when Roman showed Conrad and Inspector Chuab to the door, Jeff patted a spot on the seat beside him in invitation.

Jessica joined him, and he encircled her waist with his good arm. She leaned against him, her head resting against his shoulder.

He laid his cheek against the top of her head, and his voice sounded more at peace than any time since meeting him. "Isn't it strange how different people see the same thing and interpret it so differently?"

"You believe them then?"

"I think so."

Jessica felt a further lessening of her emotional tension. Everything was going to be all right.

"Of course," he continued, "I'll check around, but it's hard to imagine the Inspector of the Thai police *and* the head of U.S. Intelligence in Bangkok were both bought off by Roman to support his story. And if Conrad isn't who he says he is, they must know I'll find out in less time than it took them to go through their story here today. So, at least for the moment, I'll have to confess that I've witnessed something akin to a miracle. Frankly I didn't know how Roman would talk his way out of it. He certainly blew my lovely theory about the fakes at the museum, didn't he?"

"Speaking of those fakes, did you ever tell me how you became such an authority?" Jessica quizzed. "I'd be at a loss to identify a bodhisattva, pre-Ankor style, let alone tell you if it were a forgery."

"A couple of years back I tried to figure out who to make the lucky subject for my next masterpiece, and the name Samuel Lorgette kept coming to mind. You ever hear of him?"

"No," Jessica admitted and snuggled closer. She found it amazing how easy it was for her to telescope her world to include just the two of them.

"He's the art world's chief expert in separating fakes and forgeries from the real things," Jeff said. "He's the guy who told the Met their 'Portrait of a Rotterdam Burgher' wasn't a Rembrandt. He also told the Getty that their 'Ballet on a Riverbank' was no more by Degas than their 'Charioteer' was an original bronze by Phidias. I was with him one day at an art gallery in L.A. while he checked out a Buddha a museum back East had optioned to buy. He asked me if I could believe anyone would try to fob it off as genuine. When he saw I didn't know the difference, he graciously pointed out how the Buddha's topknot was all wrong, his drapery rode too high on the left side, and his eyebrows were too arched. Then, to be even kinder, he insisted that it would have been more obvious if I'd had the real thing handy as a basis of comparison. In a seeming spur-of-the-moment decision, he had me follow him to this fabulous estate in the foothills overlooking the Pacific

Ocean. The owner wasn't home, but the guards at the front gate knew Samuel and so did the butler.

In the basement he took me into a series of museum-like rooms filled with Thai artifacts. He walked me over to one in particular, a seated Buddha, and told me *that* was what the genuine article looked like. In fact, he said, there wasn't a piece there wasn't genuine, and of superior-grade to boot. He knew, because he'd been over every one with an expert's fine-tooth comb. Powell Whyte knew what he was doing when he collected them. And the way Samuel said all of that with such obvious high regard for the collector interested me in Powell Whyte for the very first time. But, if that's what hooked me, it was what he said next that buried the hook to its eye: The rumor was, you know, that it was Powell Whyte's passion for Thai art that motivated someone to kill him. I've often wondered since if he didn't do it on purpose to turn my attention to Powell and away from him."

"You think that rumor about motivation of the killer is true?" Jessica asked, because she'd heard it too. It had become part of Thailand's folklore. "Powell was out to get a particularly fine piece of Thai art, and the deal somehow went sour?"

"I'd love to know that," Jeff admitted and gave her a squeeze. "Unfortunately, I figure that's something that isn't likely to come out just to allow me a really super ending for my Powell Whyte biography."

"Anyway, I know now how you spotted the fakes in the museum," Jessica conceded.

"I decided, if I was going to write about Powell Whyte, I'd better devote some time to familiarizing myself with a subject obviously near to my subject's heart and pocketbook. Samuel helpfully gave me a number of pointers. He had studies of all the Whyte collection, as well as reproductions of several, including the two the Ron Ron happened to exchange at the museum. He took me to the mansion a couple more times, although never when Roman was in residence. I doubt Samuel wanted to have to explain about me. I did ask Samuel his opinion of Roman once. You know what he said?: 'Thank your literary stars you've got the uncle as a subject, my boy, because the nephew is Mormon, with a lily-pure reputation to boot.' Obviously, I should have known that if Roman were tainted, Samuel — or you — would have known it."

"Some things are best discovered for oneself," Jessica said, "and such discoveries warrant a nice reward. So. . ."

"Does that mean I get a kiss?" He tilted her chin with his thumb. His handsome good looks literally took her breath away, and she didn't resist when he touched his lips to hers.

The sparks cascaded through her like pyrotechnic displays produced by molten metal, spilled from huge caldrons in steel mills. They warmed the length, width, and depth of her.

"Mmmmmmm," she sighed. "I was talking reward for you, not treat for me. Something which could hopefully help you in your work."

"Oh?"

"What do you make of this?" She produced the folded piece of paper from the side pocket of her skirt.

"Whatever do we have here?" He levered himself to a more alert position as he unfolded his prize.

"I'm told there's more where that came from," Jessica said. "It can be picked up tomorrow, one o'clock, Saladang Intersection, southwest corner of Lumpini Park. He told me I have to be the envoy. All Kenneth Critzer wants to see of you is your money."

"When did you see Kenneth Critzer?" Jeff demanded, sounding as if she had done something dangerous, like swim in the klong.

"Yesterday afternoon," Jessica admitted. "Shortly after you dropped me off."

"The man is a son of a . . . ." Jeff stopped abruptly. "Well, never mind. I'm too deeply in love with a Mormon lady to indulge in vulgarity."

"Do you love me?" Jessica knew she sounded like a love-dazed schoolgirl. Then again, that was exactly how she felt, and the feeling was marvelous! "*Really* love me, I mean?"

"You dare doubt it!" he exclaimed in mock resentment.

"Okay, I believe you," she admitted softly. What's more, she loved him too and wished she could express it as easily as he did.

"You find this love downright disconcerting, don't you?"

Jessica could only nod. She was too emotion-choked to find the words.

"You've always imagined you'd fall head over heels for a staunch Mormon. Well, we agreed to take things one step at a time and look at the impressive progress we've made so far. Sometime soon, you and I will just have to sit down and have a long talk about all of this." She nodded again. "Until then," he rustled the paper she'd given him, "we'll see what it is that came from your subjecting yourself to Kenneth Critzer's company."

Although she didn't say it out loud, Jessica knew she was on the verge of a commitment, if he'd pressed her. Luckily, he apparently had sense enough to know that whatever was going on between them wasn't something to jump into with their eyes closed, especially after only three days. Neither of them were kids who could afford to approach love as a miracle cure-all.

Jeff held the paper where she could read it. "There's no doubt this can be of help to me in outlining Powell Whyte's last days," he said. "See this entry: 'B. Dilling'? That's Bradford Dilling, Vice-President of Siam Tungsten. This 'fifteen-thirty' notation for Powell to 'Call J.S.,' probably means for him to telephone either Jeremy Santu of Tompolin Lumber or Janai Siga of Whyte Silk Consortium, at three-thirty in the afternoon."

"And, 'B.O.M.,' here, here, and here?" Jessica asked. B.O.M. and Powell had met at 12:04, 14:34 and 16:16. "Don't these times strike you as a little too precise? Twelve-oh-four, not twelve, or even twelve-five?"

"Well, here's a fourteen-fifty-seven to 'Call Fondler T.,' " Jeff mused. "And, a 'Supper with R.' at twenty-oh-four. I suppose if a man considers time money, even the minutes count."

They looked up as Roman joined them, dropping gracefully into the opposing chair. "I've ordered orange juice," he said. "Also croissants, since Jessica was too nervous to eat a decent breakfast."

His words fell into a void, since neither Jeff nor Jessica had been thinking of food.

"Do you have any idea who B.O.M. might be, Roman?" Jessica asked. She felt uneasy in the momentary silence. She considered moving to one of the vacant chairs, but she simply derived far too much enjoyment from Jeff's closeness to purposely deprive herself of it.

"B.O.M.?" Roman asked curiously.

"Someone your uncle knew," Jeff said. "Powell met

him three times on. . ." He scanned the page and flipped it
over to check the other side. "Unfortunately, I can't find a
date."

"It's a page from your uncle's appointment book,"
Jessica explained to the curious Roman, glad to keep the
conversation rolling.

"His appointment book?" Roman echoed in surprise.
"Wherever from?" .

"From a sleazy source named Kenneth Critzer," Jeff
told him. "He's supposedly a nephew of Jonathan Critzer,
who was a business associate of your late Uncle Powell. He
was also killed about the same time." Jessica hoped Jeff
wouldn't reveal how she'd been responsible for obtaining
the page, since she hadn't mentioned it the night before,
and Roman's feelings might be hurt to get the word
belatedly. "Critzer wants to sell me the whole thing," Jeff
finished off to her relief.

"I didn't realize Jonathan Critzer even had a nephew."
But his tone of voice indicated the man's name rang a few
bells. When Jeff offered him the page, he took it, looking
it over with some interest. His expression was unreadable
when he finished his examination.

"Roman?" Jessica probed.

"It's not a name," he said. "B.O.M., I mean. Not the
name of a person anyway. It's a book."

"A book?" Jeff and Jessica asked in unison.

"*Book of Mormon:* B.O.M.," Roman said. "It and the
times, twelve-oh-four, fourteen-thirty-four, sixteen-
sixteen, are all part of a code Uncle Powell showed me how
to decipher when I was just a kid."

"Your Uncle Powell showed you a cipher that used the
Book of Mormon as its key?" Jessica asked. She knew
Roman was the convert. According to the rumors, Powell

Whyte had been an agnostic till the day he died.

"Remember when you once asked me what triggered my initial interest in the Church?"

"A *Book of Mormon* you found in your uncle's library, here in Thailand," Jessica recalled. "A book, one of literally hundreds of books, your uncle picked up in some Thai flea market to fill the vacant spaces on his bookshelves."

"What led me to that particular book, out of all the rest, though, was how often I spotted Uncle Powell pulling it down from the shelf."

"One day he couldn't find it and almost tore the house apart in panic. All the while I was blissfully sequestered in my room, engrossed in the tales of how Moroni fortified the line between Zarahemla and Nephi. The *Book of Mormon* was all marvelous adventure.

"Maybe as an explanation for all the fuss he made when he thought the book had been swiped by someone with more sinister motives than mine, he took me to one side and explained how, as his heir, I might as well learn, right then and there, how ciphers were sometimes necessary to keep business secrets safe from the competition. Soon he was leaving me B.O.M. codes which I'd decipher to find an extra bowl of tapioca pudding at the back of the refrigerator, or some spending money in a jar in the study, or a birthday gift in back of the bedroom closet.

"Of course, for his more important ciphers, used in business, and in private, he went on to other books. I remember, he used Anne Lindbergh's *Gift from the Sea* for a time, then Heinrich Harper's *Seven Years in Tibet* and once an espionage novel about ciphers by Ken Follet, *The Key to Rebecca*. At the time of his murder, most of his private notes, business and personnel, were ciphered from an obscure translation of an Italian biography on film-maker Enzio Pasolini. That's why these references to B.O.M. took me by surprise."

"So what do they mean?" Jessica felt her excitement rising. She also felt quite smug for having decided that there was something odd about the preciseness of writing down appointments to the minute.

"Why don't I show you," Roman suggested. "Jessica, do you have a copy of the *Book of Mormon* I could borrow?"

"I have one in my hotel room," Jeff said before she could answer.

"In your hotel room?" Jessica echoed in surprise. Occasionally she'd come across a copy in a hotel room dresser drawer, but only in Idaho or Utah. She'd never seen one during any of her stays at The Oriental Hotel.

"I had the hotel concierge drum up a copy for me late Sunday night," Jeff confessed. "Jessica inspired me to further investigate into what Mormonism is all about." He smiled wickedly and a joyful warmth stole through her body. "I just haven't found much time for reading lately."

Jessica derived a great deal of hope from Jeff's willingness to look deeper into her religious beliefs, but she couldn't disillusion herself into thinking that was the same thing as his being a Mormon. She'd once been interested enough in *nau pat prik*, beef and green pepper sauted in oyster oil, to give it a try, but she hadn't liked it. Jeff's interest in the Church offered no better guarantees.

"If yours is at the hotel, Jessica's is probably the more handy of the two," Roman suggested, interrupting her thoughts and saving Jessica from any immediate need to comment on Jeff's surprising disclosure.

"Mine will probably work," Jessica said. "Since it's not the new edition triple combination, and I suspect the book in your uncle's library wasn't either."

"Well, we'd have to make comparisons to be sure," Roman admitted. Anyway, I was thinking more along the lines of a hypothetical exercise. It's doubtful three entries are going to tell us anything of real importance, without benefit of what came before and after."

"Of course," Jessica agreed. "I'll go get my triple combination."

She found it on top of the bedroom dresser and headed back outside. The two men had moved to the glass-topped table.

"Okay," Roman said as soon as Jessica joined them. "We have a first B.O.M. entry of twelve-oh-four. So, if you'll please open your *Book of Mormon* to page twelve."

Jessica unzipped the black-leather binding and quickly found the page. "First Nephi," she said.

ye are mine elder brethren, and
how is it that ye are so hard in
your hearts

"We're interested in letters of the alphabet, punctuation marks, and the spaces after each word," Roman explained. "Twelve-oh-four means the character found on page twelve, starting the four-count from the upper left-hand corner of the main text."

"'Y' equals one; 'e' equals two," Jessica said and thought she had the knack of it. "'A' equals three; 'r' equals four."

"Except you need to count the space after 'ye,'" Roman said. "We count all spaces and punctuation marks, remember."

"'Space' equals three," Jessica amended. "'A' equals four?" she concluded but made it a question.

"'A' it is! So, you see, we're not talking anything too complicated here, as long as we know which book is used as the key. The same four-count on page twelve of, say, *War and Peace,* would give us an entirely different letter."

"So, B.O.M. fourteen-thirty-four gives us what?" Jeff asked. He checked the page from the appointment book to pinpoint the next pertinent cipher entry.

"Page fourteen," Jessica said and flipped a page. "Still First Nephi."

> *and at the head thereof I beheld*
> *your mother, Sariah, and Sam,*
> *and Nephi*

"Deciphering to what?" Roman encouraged.

Jessica counted out the characters. "Y."

"We have an 'a' and a 'Y,' then," Jeff said. "And, feeling like a contestant on 'Wheel of Fortune,' shall we all move on from here—to sixteen-sixteen?"

Again Jessica flipped the page.

> *hath all power unto the fulfilling*
> *of all his words*

"'U,'" she said.

"'A,' 'y,' 'u,'" Jeff said. "Giving us what?"

"Not much," Roman admitted. "The beginning of a word? The middle of a word? The ending of a word? Maybe not even that if the format of this *Book of Mormon* isn't printed in exactly the same layout as the one back at the house. And without the rest of the cipher entries, we have nothing."

"We do know where the rest are, don't we?" Jessica said, reminding them all that most of the mystery had yet to be solved. "At least, we know where they'll be tomorrow at one o'clock sharp."

"Where?" Roman asked.

"Saladang Intersection, at the southwest corner of Lumpini Park," Jessica said. "And I say we go for it!"

10

"You know, you needn't go through with this," Jeff said. Jessica sat between him and Roman in a taxi parked on Rajadamri Road across ..rom the Royal Bangkok Sport Club Race Track. Except for a brief stop at a jewelry store, they'd come directly from a memorial service for Tim Spencer, from which Conrad Tiller, Tim's immediate supervisor at the Embassy, had been surprisingly absent.

Two long blocks ahead, hardly visible, was the Saladang Intersection where Rajadamri Road met Rama IV Road and converted to Silom Road on the other side. The trees of Lumpini Park were visible far forward and off to the left.

"Not go through with it?" That was the farthest thing from her mind. "You must be kidding! I appreciate a good mystery as much as anyone, especially one with secret ciphers and possible treasure waiting at the end."

"I just thought I detected a hint of hesitation," Jeff apologized. Grinning, he checked his watch.

At the same time, Jessica checked hers, an elegantly-styled new gold Piaget, with a simple black leather band. The watch was one Jessica had been tempted to buy her last two times to the city, and there had seemed no time like the present to give herself a reward, no matter the expense, for having survived this far. Especially with her old one ruined.

"Actually, I was just thinking how a *Book of Mormon*, picked up by Powell Whyte at random in a Bangkok flea market, is responsible for Roman's conversion to Mormonism, and for us ending up here."

"And I was just thinking how odd it remains that Kenneth Critzer ended up with my uncle's appointment book," Roman injected. "For the life of me, I can't recall Jonathan Critzer ever having had a nephew."

"I didn't have any luck making that family connection, either," Jeff admitted, "but I suppose it's possible."

"Maybe it was because Kenneth wasn't all that well-known that his uncle turned the book over to him for safekeeping," Jessica ventured. She refused to believe they didn't have something here that portended a pot of gold at the end of the rainbow. This unraveling of the mysterious cipher would have been the most exciting thing in her life, if it didn't have so many exciting things with which to contend lately.

"Which brings us to the interesting question of how Jonathan Critzer happened to have my uncle's appointment book to pass on to Kenneth in the first place," Roman said.

"Well, it's about time for Jessica to leave," Jeff said with another check of his watch.

Smiling with an odd sense of expectation, Jessica turned to Roman. "So, wish me luck!"

"Luck," he said, opening the door to get out.

When she turned to Jeff, he lightly touched her cheek. "If the jerk lays a finger on even one hair of your head, he'll have both Roman and me to answer to personally." She heard the emotion in his voice, and her surging adrenalin increased. She leaned toward him, and he captured her lips. The kiss was brief and exhilerating. She knew the strength of it would carry her through the adventure yet to come.

"Wait until you see how fast I'm back for repeats," she promised, bracing the back of his neck with her hand and kissing him again quickly.

He left the cab but signalled the thumb's-up sign and as soon as the door closed between them, the car started up. Jessica looked back and waved. Neither man looked pleased at his exclusion from the proceedings, but Jessica knew she could handle the exchange on her own. If Kenneth did try to pull a fast one on the crowded Bangkok street, Jeff had assured Jessica that the hand-picked driver of her cab would be somewhere close by to lend her a hand.

The maze of walkways, trees, and lakes that made up Lumpini Park, one of the few public oases of greenery in a city of over four-million people, loomed on her left. When the park formed an obtuse angle that paralleled Saladang Intersection, Jessica got out.

She adjusted the strap of her purse on her shoulder to position it securely under her arm. She wouldn't give Kenneth even the slightest chance to come away from this with something for nothing.

However, it wasn't Kenneth who approached her from

within the first flood of pedestrians to engulf her. "I believe you have something for me, Miss Miller," said a man who was Chinese and half Kenneth's size. His total weight might have matched Kenneth's, but it was put to far better advantage on the Chinese man's smaller frame.

"If you're Kenneth Critzer, you're to be congratulated on your disguise," Jessica said.

"I'm afraid Mr. Critzer couldn't come," he said without a hint of a smile at Jessica's attempt at humor. "He did, however, send me with this." He took the appointment book out of the brown shopping bag he carried, fanning the pages of the book so Jessica could clearly see the handwritten entries made in Powell Whyte's distinctive scrawl. "In return, I assume you have something for me."

She took the envelope out of her purse and deftly exchanged it for the book. Actually, she was glad Kenneth was too paranoid for a personal appearance. Something about him gave her the creeps.

"One minute, please!" the man insisted before she could melt away through the crowd and find her taxi.

The Chinese man broke the sealed flap of the envelope and brazenly counted the money, needless of the throng of people. Once satisfied, he performed a disappearing act that would have done Oliver Twist proud.

Jessica blinked to make sure he was really gone, then checked to make sure he hadn't taken the appointment book with him. Reassured that she still possessed it, she went to the curb and waved away two taxis and a tuk tuk before the driver that had dropped her off returned to take her away.

Less than ten minutes later, she was back where she'd left Jeff and Roman. She found Nikolas waiting for them with the limousine.

"Success!" she announced, holding the appointment book high in evidence. "Let's be off to find the treasure!"

"Short detour first," Jeff said, disappointing Jessica with an all-too-brief congratulatory kiss. "The police got enough out of Hua Deng to locate the warehouse the Ron Ron group used to store its contraband. The Ron Ron were scrambling like mad to relocate when Inspector Chuab arrived on the scene."

"Han Anyank was killed, and two of his chief lieutenants were wounded," Roman said. "So it looks as if the Ron Ron's heads have been lopped off, hopefully to put the beast out of action."

"Fantastic!" Jessica exclaimed. She didn't doubt for a minute that the terrorists got what they deserved.

"It's not far to the warehouse." Roman motioned for Jessica and Jeff to enter the car through the door Nikolas held open for them. They barely had time to give the appointment book an enticing cursory once-over before the car stopped amid a clutter of police cars and ramshackled buildings grouped on the edge of the river. Inspector Chuab emerged from one of the buildings. Conrad Tiller followed close behind.

"The last of the wounded were removed a couple of minutes ago," Inspector Chuab said by way of greeting. "All those in any condition for talking have been routed to the station for questioning." He motioned for them to come inside. "Now, we're trying to get a handle on all of this." A wave of his arm encompassed the artifacts that filled the building to capacity.

Jessica was both surprised and impressed by the extent of the contraband. There seemed to be enough artifacts to fill three museums.

"Originals *and* forgeries, I see." Jeff paced down the

line of excess Buddhas, seated and standing, bronze, brass, porphyry, and limestone; Devi and Siva statues and statuettes; headless, armless, and legless rock torsos; Ardhanari heads; votive plaques; sandstone figures of Uma, Vishnu, Hanuman, and Prajnaparamita.

"Through here is something of particular interest to the three of you." Conrad steered the party through a labyrinth of passageways that led deeper into the rabbit warren of metal and stone figures. The preponderance of inanimate objects gave Jessica the uneasy feeling she had somehow been made just another piece in a complicated Oriental chess game.

Conrad stopped them before two bodhisattvas. "Look familiar?"

"The originals from the museum," Jeff identified immediately.

Suddenly a voice called from deep within the warehouse. "Inspector Chuab! It looks like we have a. . ."

He never said "bomb" because the explosion said it for him. An ear-deafening chain reaction roared through the complex, toppling artwork like dominoes.

Jeff grabbed Jessica's hand, pulling her toward the exit. In the melee she lost track of Roman and the others, and the world seemed to be falling around her.

The floor rolled like jello, and they entered a narrow passageway. Jessica collided with a wobbly wooden statue. She lost her balance in the collision and went down, losing her grip on Jeff's hand. Simultaneously, a blinding sunburst of white-hot light and hellish flames went off on her right, and Jeff stumbled backwards as shelves of pottery and standing Buddhas toppled in unison. Jessica struggled to her feet, but Jeff was lost in the ten-foot pile of new rubble.

11

"Jeff?" she called, listening desperately for his response. When she didn't hear one, she hurriedly backtracked in an attempt to find some way around to him. She couldn't bear the thought he might have been killed.

She called him again and again, distracted only when a resounding crack singled itself out from the general pandemonium. She turned toward the sound and watched a wooden platform complete its collapse with another loud crack that spilled a large bronze statue of a demon, as if intent upon making Jessica its victim.

Defensively, she lifted her arms, although she knew the statue was heavy enough to crush her. Her palms flattened against bronze, but she staggered under its weight, falling, falling until her shoulders and head banged sharply against the floor.

Then, with a thud, the statue stopped just short of

hitting her. Jessica didn't ask herself why. She knew why. The Lord was looking over her. And her opinion didn't change when she squeezed out from under and saw how the demon's sword had split the wooden Buddha, its blade stuck in the wooden base only three feet short of the floor.

Jessica said a prayer of thanks but knew the meaning of, "Out of the frying pan, into the fire," because there was fire all around her. The heat sucked sweat from her pores. The flames hurt her eyes and skin. The greed of the fire deprived her of oxygen. The roar drowned all other sounds.

A metal Vishnu atop the metal Garuna bird he rode, seemed to glow in the furnace-like heat. A figure of Chanda-li seemed to dance within a shower of sparks. The figure of a Brahmin turned blackamoor beneath a fallout of greasy soot.

It was a Hades-like maze complicated by fallen statues and debris that seemed to block all exits. She was forced to take whatever path was open to her. She stepped over the dented metal of a multi-armed Prajnaparamita and squeezed around the large stone head of a decapitated Dhammapala.

She no longer called Jeff. Just breathing was a chore in the scorching heat and the increasing smoke. But she didn't stop looking for him under every fallen statue or beneath every tumbled piece of debris.

Had she been in top physical condition, she would have given herself a better chance for survival. As it was, constantly bombarded by traumas over the last few days, her body hadn't had a chance to recuperate from even one trial before being subjected to yet another. If she were a fighter, and she was, there was only so much fighting she could do. There came a time in everyone's life when the

Lord called, no second chances allowed.

She leaned against hot stone that might have been part of a seated Buddha lost in the murk and gloom. Her brain in low gear, it slowly dawned on her that the air on her face was less searing than it had been.

She turned to confront a smoky breeze that reached her over a terra-cotta deer whose folded legs gave it the collapsed appearance of a poor animal that had succumbed to asphyxiation. She moved forward past a limestone Hari-Hara whose two left arms, one hand holding a seashell, laid broken at the figure's feet.

Jessica sensed escape; however, the way to that escape remained hidden from her by a river of smoke that was getting thicker by the second. If she didn't know what awaited her within and beyond the smoke, her desperation drove her to risk whatever was necessary rather than stay helplessly where she was. Realizing sadly that she was no longer in any condition to save Jeff, even if she found him, she surrendered to her survival instincts, held her breath, and plunged forward. Desperately, she tried to see through the smoke while soot and ash clogged her pores and irritated her fire-dried mouth and nose.

She didn't know how long she could hold her breath, or how long she could keep going.

Her legs, which had carried her to the limits of their endurance, collapsed, and she fell to her knees. Despite the painful telescoping of her spine, and the jarring impact of her teeth, she found the position wonderfully suitable for giving thanks for her escape. Apparently a hole had been blown through the warehouse wall by one of the earlier explosions, and fresh air now cascaded into her smoke-weary lungs.

"Jessica!"

She wanted it to be Jeff who called her, but it wasn't. Still, she didn't begrudge Roman his survival.

For the first time since she'd known him, his hair was awry, his suit tattered and torn, streaked with shades of dirty gray. He dropped beside her on the ash-covered ground, took her in his arms, and drew her head to his shoulder. "Jeff's safe, too," he told her, holding her tightly. It was what she most wanted to hear, and she heaved sobs of joyful relief.

"Thank you, Father!" Jessica said through her tears, completely surrendering her rattled emotions to a good cry.

Roman offered her his soot-covered handkerchief, and his smile identified his offer as an attempt at levity.

She smiled back at him through the day. "I never thought I'd see the day Roman Whyte couldn't come up with a clean handkerchief for a lady in distress." She wiped her eyes with the backs of her hands, which probably did a better job than the hanky could have.

He helped her to her feet. "Last I saw Jeff, he was being given oxygen for smoke inhalation at one of the aid stations."

But, it was Jeff who found them, and his resulting embrace took Jessica's breath away.

Joyously happy, she wrapped her arms around his neck and hung on while he twirled her. The moment demanded slow-motion camera work and an alpine meadow overflowing with bluebells.

"Thank God you're safe!" Jeff exclaimed, giving her the smoke-flavored kiss she so eagerly wanted. "I thought I'd lost you!" He kissed her again.

In an equivalent of the fireworks that went off at such moments in the movies, the warehouse roof collapsed with a bang.

"What a waste!" Roman said. "Incendiary bombs placed there by an obsessed mentality. Believe me, the world is better off with the Ron Ron out of commission. Such groups are a genuine menace to civilized society."

"Amen!" agreed a frazzled looking Inspector Chuab who joined them. Before Jessica could ask about Conrad Tiller, the inspector said, "No sign of Conrad or three of my best men. Just when we think we've made a little headway, something like this happens. Two steps forward, one back. That's the way it goes."

He gave them leave to go, saying he'd know where to find them.

Nikolas waited at the limousine, his smoke-streaked face and clothes indicating he hadn't waited idly by. His right hand was wrapped in a rag of dirty cloth, but he insisted he could drive.

Jessica got out at the Simms's compound after everyone agreed they'd meet there for an early supper, unless the events of the day finally caught up with them.

After a muscle-relaxing hot bath once again, Jessica experienced her marvelous recuperative powers. Roman and Jeff obviously had just as much luck, because they turned up at six o'clock sharp and looked only a little the worst for wear.

They dined on *laph*, a Laotian dish of minced chicken, mint, shallots, and dry *prik kee nu* peppers. It was spicy without blowing off the tops of their heads, and it arrived with hot fresh rolls and side dishes of snow peas and little ears of yellow corn. Jessica always wondered if the latter were grown in bonsai cornfields.

Afterwards, they retired to the study with Powell Whye's appointment book and the *Book of Mormon*

Roman brought from his house.

"I wonder how things might be different if Uncle Powell had spent more time reading this *Book of Mormon* instead of using it as a key for his ciphers?" Roman mused as they settled down to see what Powell Whyte had left for them hidden among his entries.

"Maybe he got more out of the book than you know," Jeff suggested. "The details of his will say his decision to return the collection to the Thai people was a carefully thought out one and not exactly deathbed repentance."

"Keep saying such things, and I might be won over to Jessica's theory that you're prepared to render an objective accounting of my uncle's life," Roman said. Jeff apparently thought that enough of a concession not to make any comment.

There followed three hours of intense concentration, punctuated at the end of a completed decipherment of the B.O.M. entries by Roman's announcement, "We may not know what we have, but we certainly know where to find it, don't we?"

"Where" was Ayudhaya, about forty-five miles north of Bangkok. Once the national capital of Thailand, the city had been founded in 1351 and nearly destroyed by a Burmese invasion in 1767. Jessica had once visited the old city which was now nine-square miles of jungle-overgrown collapsed masonry, crumbled pavilions, and toppled spires.

At eight o'clock the next morning, Jessica, Jeff, and Roman boarded one of the Whyte company's helicopters, destination Ayudhaya, Nikolas at the controls. They could have driven, or gone by boat, but flying was more convenient and took less time.

"I told my secretary that Jessica has a bolt of silk to pick up at the lab outside Kumpu-wapi," Roman said, strapping himself in. "If this treasure hunt doesn't pan out, we can do just that, since Ayudhaya is on the way. I said Jeff was coming along because I was reconsidering cooperation on his book, and he'd find the lab of interest for background."

"*Are* you reconsidering?" Jeff asked, obviously unable to let the query pass.

"If I am," Roman vacillated, "please remember that doesn't necessarily mean cooperation."

"Right!" Jeff said, but Jessica could tell he was pleased. She was too.

The ruins were nearly deserted because most tourists would arrive later by boat. If the particular pavilion for which they looked was less conspicuous and grand than the 400-foot "Golden Mount," a pyramid surmounted by a domed spire, it was nonetheless almost as easy to locate because Roman had pinpointed the building on a detailed map of Ayudhaya found in his library at home.

Knowing where the door to the building should be, though, and finding it wasn't the same thing. Collapsed masonry had converted a full door into a miniscule crawl-way.

Roman dropped to his hands and knees and poked his flashlight through the opening. "Plenty of room on the other side."

They entered a stairwell that went downward. A Coleman lantern proved invaluable lighting, and Jessica was glad Roman had had the forethought to bring it along.

Jessica's foot dislodged a large piece of the stair, and Jeff's assistance in maintaining her balance allowed her to continue enjoying the sense of adventure. She was glad recent events hadn't jaded her to simple pleasures.

The stairs ended in a room too big for the Coleman lantern to light completely. High above, tiny openings in the ceiling provided laser-like beams that crisscrossed without ever reaching the bottom.

"Looks like someone was here before us," Roman observed. Even in the light available, they saw obvious evidence of extensive trenching. "However, none of the turned dirt smells all that fresh."

"Whoever was here went to a lot of trouble for nothing," Nikolas observed.

"At least we can hope it was for nothing," Jeff amended.

Jessica located a massive square of stone off to one side. No matter what Powell Whyte's deciphered message guaranteed, Jessica wasn't in the least convinced that anything but heavy equipment could budge that block of granite.

Powell's instructions seemed contradictory at this point; so much so that they'd been gone over it more than once to make sure they'd been deciphered correctly. As it stood, someone was supposed to sit on the southeast corner of the slab, thereby providing additional weight, while someone else pushed counterclockwise on the northwest corner.

Jeff sat and Roman pushed, and Jessica wasn't the only one surprised when, without an audible grunt from Roman, the whole slab rotated a quick couple of inches.

"Seems stuck," Roman announced shortly after their initial success. "Nikolas?" he asked for help.

Nikolas gave a hand, then a shoulder, both to no apparent avail.

"Maybe it's moved all it's supposed to," Jessica

ventured, and her flashlight pinpointed how one corner of
the slab had moved sufficiently off its base to reveal a fist-
sized hole in the stone underneath. Jessica knelt and pulled
a leather pouch from the hole.

"Definitely not bigger than a bread box," Jeff
observed, coming down from his perch. Immediately, the
whole block of granite, without human assistance, shifted
back to its original position.

The four silently savored their anticipation.

"Well, Jessica," Jeff said finally. "We now know it's a
pouch. The question remains: 'Is there a kangaroo inside
it?'"

Jessica put her flashlight down and opened the draw-
strings. She reached inside and touched something so hard
and cold that she jerked her hand back out.

"Clue two: it bites," Jeff said, and Jessica felt the
resurgence of confidence necessary to try again.

Everyone audibly gasped appreciation at the results of
her efforts, and Nikolas asked, "Is that what I think it is?"

The square-cut gem, the size of a playing card, was the
same exquisite shade of green as the bolt of silk that
awaited Jessica in Kumpu-wapi. Engraved into it was the
image of a seated Buddha.

"If you think it's an emerald with Buddha intaglio,
you're correct," Kenneth Critzer said, emerging with gun in
hand from the deeper shadows.

"Been waiting a frustratingly long time for this
moment, have you, Kenneth?" Roman asked. He seemed
far less surprised to see the repulsive man than Jessica was.
"That is if Kenneth Critzer is your real name."

"Oh, it's Kenneth, all right, but not Critzer," the
gunman confessed, "but, 'What's in a name?' as old Will
Shakespeare would say."

"No matter the name, you killed Jonathan Critzer and my uncle, didn't you!"

"The emerald should have been mine in the first place," Kenneth said. "The man who killed the ignorant Thai peasant who found it was my man, but he figured Jonathan Critzer could offer him bigger bucks for it, because Critzer had Powell Whyte's sizable bank account behind him. I followed the double-dealing snake when he came here to meet Critzer and Whyte and hand over the stone. I killed him on his way out, and I helped myself to the money they'd paid him. I went back for the emerald itself when Critzer and Whyte didn't seem all that anxious to come out of here with it. Actually, I figured they might have skipped out with it through some other exit, and that made me angry and more than a little nervous. So angry and so nervous, as a matter of fact, I'm afraid I killed them, all the while thinking, 'Why *not* eliminate all witnesses?' I was sure my man had brought the emerald in. On the other hand, neither Critzer nor Whyte had the gem when I searched their bodies before hauling them elsewhere for dumping. As one of you so eruditely commented earlier, I've spent a good deal of my time and effort since then looking for it."

"And my uncle's appointment book?" Roman asked.

"He had it with him," Kenneth said. "So I kept it. Originally, I figured it might have something important to tell me if I could read between the mundane lines. However, by the time I approached Billings, it wasn't because I expected him to find answers I couldn't, but because I needed money to get me out of the country as a result of a soured business deal. Holding onto the book wasn't doing me any good, and I figured Billings would be able to use it as a reference source for his research.

Luckily, I decided to stick around a while, just in case he suddenly headed in this direction after he got it. Wasn't I surprised by just how fast that exodus from Bangkok occurred?"

Suddenly Inspector Chuab appeared from the shadows, delivering a chop with his pistol across Kenneth's extended gun hand that persuaded Kenneth to drop his gun.

"You broke my wrist!"

Jessica was surprised it was over so quickly.

"Word on the street is that Kenneth Leland here accepted several stolen artifacts from the Ron Ron not too long ago," said Inspector Chuab. "Right Kenneth? Kenneth rather fancies himself an antiques broker of sorts, and he isn't above a bit of wheeling and dealing. Including the exchange of some munitions for some ill-gotten statues the Ron Ron had in storage until recently. Trouble was he gave them guns that didn't work the way they were supposed to because Kenneth's source for the guns had pulled a fast one. The Ron Ron came back for redress and got their artifacts back before Kenneth could market them, but they missed bagging Kenneth. Since then, we and the Ron Ron have both been on the outlook for him. Too bad for Kenneth that this meeting comes after we've broken up the Ron Ron, because he now has very little with which to bargain. I wonder, Kenneth, did you think we made the world a safer place by eliminating the Ron Ron when it would have only been a matter of time before they got to you?"

"I'd like to know why he assumed I'd swallow his bull about being Jonathan Critzer's nephew without checking it out," Roman said.

"Oh, I don't think he ever expected you even to come

into it," Inspector Chuab told him. "Or, if you did, not nearly as quickly. He was dealing with Jeff, remember, who was liable to be a bit more accepting of the story. At the time you were telling Jeff to keep his distance. Obviously Kenneth should have been less greedy and skipped the country with the money Jeff gave him for the appointment book. I figure he got overconfident when he heard how we'd taken care of his Ron Ron problem. Is that the way it was, Kenneth? Did you forget that people clever enough to put the Ron Ron out of commission would certainly be able to deal with small-time scum like you?"

Inspector Chuab pulled out his handcuffs, and Jessica, who still remembered the indignity she'd suffered by having been handcuffed to the door of Kenneth's blue van, couldn't have been more pleased by the poetic justice.

The next day, Roman decided to give Jeff full cooperation on the Powell Whyte biography. "Jessica got me thinking that we all have to stand on our own merits and shouldn't be held responsible for the faults of others. Besides, I truly believe Uncle Powell's favorable qualities outweigh his bad, if only because he did so much to give Thailand's economy the impetus that keeps it healthy to this day. If he made mistakes, he also made a conscious effort to right some of them by returning the artwork he'd misappropriated in his lifetime. I think, if given all the facts, few people will label him an incorrigible villain."

Jeff and Roman spent the day going through Powell Whyte's papers, and they joined Jessica for supper at Chit Pochana on Sukhumuit Road.

Jessica hadn't spent the day doing nothing, either. She created several new design possibilities that might do justice to the bolt of silk still awaiting her in Kumpu-wapi.

But never far from conscious thought was Jeff. Could this really be love after such a short time? And where could their relationship lead? She was thirty-six and wanted to be married, but after waiting all this time could she give up her goal of a Temple marriage and marry a nonmember?

Saturday began with a flight to Kumpu-wapi to get the silk. Seeing yards of it at once made Jessica reject every design as inadequate, and she didn't mind. For this silk only something very special would do. At the plant Roman gave the others a fascinating tour of the facilities which were gearing up to mass-produce the new green dye.

Then they hurried to Bangkok for the gala festivities to christen the completed Powell Whyte Memorial Museum.

There were two separate private receptions scheduled as lead-ins to the night's main event. The first was one in which Roman, representing his uncle's estate, was to be presented to the King and Queen of Thailand. The invitation was extended to include Jeff and Jessica who had agreed, along with Roman to make the newly-acquired emerald-with-Buddha-intaglio a permanent part of the museum's collection. The second was one in which the top-ranking Thai members of the museum staff would be presented to their King and Queen.

"That division," explained Roman, "has nothing to do with race or status, by the way, but with a concentrated effort to make us Americans feel as comfortable as possible; foreigners, born and raised in democracies, are often disconcerted by Thai protocol that still requires Thai subjects to approach Their Majesties on all fours, not to mention address the royal presence in a special, elaborate language, *Rachasap*, that aims all conversation indirectly to the 'coarse visible dust,' and the 'fine invisible dust, under the soles of Their Majesties' feet.'

"Such concessions to us probably come far easier to this King then it did to his less worldly-wise predecessors; although the British, who arrived in Thailand quite early, set the precedent for foreigners *not* going prostrate before Thai kings—the British refusing to go all that far even before their own royals."

"Your efforts on behalf of the Thai silk industry are well-known to us, Miss Miller," King Bhumibol Adulyadej told her in excellent English that hinted of his birth in the United States when his father attended Harvard.

The King was in a dark, double-breasted dinner jacket of Thai silk, tuxedo pants, a plain, unruffled dress shirt, and black bow tie. His cufflinks were gold-enclosed circlets of onyx. He stood ramrod straight, his expression unsmilingly serious, beads of sweat across his high forehead.

Queen Sirikit's demeanor was less strait-laced, but that might have been because she'd met everyone but Jeff before. The Queen, an avid promoter of Thai handiwork, had toured one of the Whyte Silk Consortium weaving facilities the year before, and Roman, on friendly terms with both Their Majesties, had, at that time, introduced Jessica as another eager promoter of Thai silk.

"It's nice to see you again, Miss Miller," the Queen greeted, her handshake warmly welcoming. "Your dress is exquisite. One of your own designs, I presume?" Jessica confessed it was and, without saying so, knew she could have done far better for Her Majesty than the locally designed and locally made high-collared gown of heavy brocade the Queen wore. "I'll be in New York next April. . ." Queen Sirikit said. Having read Jessica's critical thoughts? ". . . and I'd very much like to see your salon."

"I'd be more than pleased to receive you," Jessica graciously replied.

"I suppose there are certain publicity advantages, and snob appeal, to 'dressing' the Queen of Thailand in a Jessica Miller original," Jeff whispered, his arm slipping around Jessica's waist as Their Majesties proceeded into the adjoining room to be greeted with far less informality by their Thai subjects.

Shortly, thereafter, everyone joined the bulk of the guests in the main room for speeches, followed by a buffet-dinner dance. Neither the King nor the Queen stayed for the latter.

"Do you think it's because we Americans, and all the Europeans present, would expect His Majesty to gallop around the dance floor as Yul Brynner did with Deborah Kerr in 'The King and I'?" Jessica asked as, with a hand on each of Jeff's shoulders, she went gliding around the dance floor with him. His one arm still in a sling, Jeff expertly used his good hand, firmly positioned in the small of Jessica's back, to lead her skillfully through the intricacies of the Viennese waltz. She knew classical Thai dances would have been entirely inappropriate for such an internationally mixed social occasion; they were highly stylized and, more often than not, required participants to "become" monkeys, or other esoteric characters from *The Ramakien.*

"Well, 'The King and I' has been banned in Thailand for a good many years," Jeff said and led Jessica into yet another series of tight whirls that made her green-silk ball gown rustle sensuously as it shifted fluidly around her body-in-motion. "I suppose your Brynner-Kerr explanation is as good as the historical-anomaly explanation most often used as the chief reason for instigating and maintaining the ban."

"Mmmmmm," Jessica replied and forgot all about Yul and Deborah. Rather, she succumbed to the rhythm and flow of the dance and lost herself in Jeff's arms. She hummed the "Blue Danube" as it was simultaneously played by the Bangkok Musicians' Strauss Appreciation Society.

"Do you know we won't know each other even a full week until tomorrow morning?" she asked, even more securely telescoping her world to include only Jeff, the waltz, and herself.

"Then why does it seem as if I've known and loved you for a lifetime?" he asked, and he gave her a twirl that took her breath away.

"Tomorrow is Sunday," she said, and she was acutely aware of his strong shoulders beneath the cool silk of his black tuxedo jacket. "An anniversary of sorts," she reminded, and her desire to ask him to join her at Sunday services was detoured by Roman who picked that precise moment to cut in.

"You look absolutely radiant," Roman said and made it a mild accusation. He took up the dance where Jeff left off, and he did so with a smoothness and skill that defied anyone, Jessica included, to remember the waltz's flow had been interrupted.

From there on out, the night, for Jessica, became an endless merry-go-round ride that swept her round and round the room, guided, with varying degrees of Fred Astaire expertise, by Roman, the British Ambassador, the Thai Prime Minister, the Italian aide-de-camp, the French charge d'affaires, and any number of other witty, urbane, sophisticated, and handsome gentlemen, who could charm and amuse without saying anything memorable.

Each time Jeff returned to claim her, Jessica knew what pure pleasure was all about. If she remained determined, each time, to ask him, straight out, to go to church with her the next day, the right moment to do so kept evading her.

In the end, when she finally had him completely to herself, at the door of the Simms's house, weak from his good-night kiss, she let that final opportunity slip by her too, because she suddenly realized, with a sinking heart, that, had he wanted to come to church with her, he'd had plenty of time to volunteer, without her having to spell out what he had to have known she wanted.

Her dream-like euphoria thereby tainted by Jeff not having taken the unvoiced cue to make her evening perfect, Jessica closed the door slowly between them. In doing so, she wondered if she'd be forever regretful if she didn't immediately put him on the other side of an even bigger, thicker, and stronger barrier.

12

Sunday morning, after a night of twisting and turning, Jessica stretched for the alarm as the bedroom door opened to admit the maid with a tray of freshly squeezed orange juice, toast, and scrambled eggs, plus the morning English-language paper that pictured Roman, Jeff, and Jessica predominately featured on the front page.

Throughout breakfast, she refused to face the problem that bothered her. She didn't face it in the shower either, and for once, she came out of the water no more refreshed than when she'd entered it.

She dressed in a Jessica Miller rose-colored linen suit, heels and accessories to match. She had the houseboy call a cab and waited in the garden.

It was Jeff's polite cough that told her he'd joined her while she was mentally berating herself for sidestepping, for so long, the fact that his not being a member of the Church had been an obstacle to her happiness from the very beginning.

"Jeff?!" she exclaimed, as if her thoughts had conjured a phantom who merely looked like Jeff in his silk suit the color of clotted cream, his pale beige shirt, and his tie whose paisley design mirrored the cream and the beige.

"I'm pleased you haven't forgotten," Jeff said and smiled his marvelous smile; Jessica didn't know when she'd ever seen any man so startlingly handsome. Then, he said to her the very same thing he'd said the first time they'd met in the lobby of The Oriental Hotel only a short week ago. "I understand you're attending Latter-day Saint church services this morning, and I'd like to tag along, if I may. I confess that I find Bangkok streets somewhat daunting."

He reached for her hand, and she gave it willingly. He kissed her fingertips, and as only he could make her feel, she experienced pleasurable shivers.

She slid her free hand around his neck and buried her fingers in his silky hair. His eyes were so velvety brown, his dimple so deep, his lips so inviting.

"It seems I've fallen hopelessly in love with this Mormon lady," he said, "and a good friend of hers told me, in no uncertain terms, that my not being a Mormon could cause problems. So, I've just this morning called the president of a certain Thai branch to see if he could arrange for me to meet with a couple of Mormon missionaries, because I don't know nearly enough about your church as I need to know."

"You can't change religions as easily as you change hats," Jessica warned, although the fact that he hadn't promised any definite religious commitment before he heard the lessons assured her of his sincerity more than his profession of instantaneous conversion would have done.

"One step at a time has certainly worked for us so far, wouldn't you say?" he argued and pulled her in tight. If she were afraid of hurting his arm, still in its sling, he didn't seem to share her concern. "What do you say we just continue, one step at a time?" he suggested, "encouraged by the fact that I'm not presently affiliated with any formal religious body from which my apostasy will prove all that traumatic? What's more, what I do know about Mormonism has impressed me. For instance, I genuinely like the idea of marriage for time and eternity. You know why?" He didn't let her answer but gave her a quick kiss before he answered his own question. "I like it, because I can't imagine a mere lifetime with you as being nearly enough."

"I love you," she whispered, and even the dirty klong, glimpsed through the breaks in the Litchi trees, sparkled like rare and luminescent topaz.

"And, have *I* told *you* lately that I love you?" he asked just before Jessica's lips sealed his with a kiss.

It was a hot, radiant sun, but not a Bangkok sun. Nor was the gold, telegraphing the rays of that sun, the gold on the roof of any pagan Bangkok pavilion. The trees were stately palms, but not Bangkok palms; and, the sky, in backdrop, was a more glorious azure than the liquid blue of any steamy Bangkok sky an ocean away.

This was a Los Angeles sun, and the gold was the gold of Moroni atop the Los Angeles Temple. The palms were L.A. palms grouped beside the tiered steps on which Jessica and Jeff posed for their picture; and, the blue L.A. sky was the miracle of wind and special meteorological conditions that had momentarily swept away murky, overcast, gray-brown smog to make the day as perfect as those when pollution-free orange groves stretched from horizon to horizon.

"Got it!" Roman announced.

He stepped back, and Jessica was so surprised when Jeff swooped in to scoop her into his strong arms that she gave a delighted squeal.

"Are you happy, Mrs. Billings?" he asked and kept her held tightly in his arms.

"On the first day of forever, who wouldn't be happy, Mr. Billings?" she reminded, and, her mouth coming open beneath the pressure of his kiss, she felt the all-familiar, but nonetheless ecstatic, tingling that electrified her all of the way to the tips of her toes.

The End

Letter from the Editor. . .

Dear Readers,

Didn't you enjoy Janet's article in last month's newsletter? She had a wonderful idea — a hero of the month — that I'd like to implement. Please describe your nominee in 500 words or less. We'll publish the winning entries in the newsletter and the authors of the winning letters will each receive a book. I found Janet's husband Tom to be genuinely heroic, and I'm certainly anxious to learn about your own personal heroes.

One reader sent me a copy of a terrific magazine, *BBW (Big Beautiful Women)*. She works in a bookstore in Southern California, and she says that she and many of the Heritage Romance readers are *BBW*. Why shouldn't we have a heroine who is one also? Agreed.

Cory Stewart has worked hard to establish a successful interior decorating company. Now after eight years, she is having a real vacation — a trip to Greece. But nothing goes right. She spills her purse at Customs; the hotel has failed to reserve her a room; she overhears a sinister conversation; and a car nearly runs her down. Is this coincidence? Or has she stumbled into a dangerous plot? Why does John Marcusen keep turning up? Is he friend or foe? If you enjoy romantic suspense, don't miss *The Antoinette Rubies* by Pat Hanson in August. An excerpt is included in this book.

Janet has another book coming out in October, *Serenade for Serenity*. Willa has traveled throughout the world and is writing a book set in each of the seven continents. The next one, which will be released in January 1988, takes place in South America. Africa is also scheduled. The plots are all unusual and page-turners!

I love receiving your letters, so if you have comments or ideas of things we might do to improve HERITAGE ROMANCES, please let us know. Don't forget authors are available to speak to groups.

I hope you're having a wonderful summer. Now that school's out I have a chance to catch up on all my correspondence and read manuscripts. Sometime during the summer I am hoping for a break to do some reading that isn't potential HERITAGE ROMANCES or galleys. The long days of summer make this my favorite season of the year. I hope you accomplish your goals this summer, too.

Best wishes,

Beverly

Beverly King

The Antoinette Rubies

by

Pat Hanson

Behind Cory, the sharp metal click of the door lock registered abruptly in the whirling confusion of her thoughts. Only a few minutes ago she had been sure the earrings were not hers. Now, this pleasant Greek with his flawless English and impeccable clothing had swept away her last certainty in this whole muddled, frightening day. Disoriented, she stood on the sidewalk staring after the man as he disappeared around a corner.

"You shouldn't frown like that, you know. It's strictly forbidden in Athena's city."

The deep masculine voice startled her, and she wheeled around. Mr. Marcusen leaned casually against the white-washed wall of the shop, looking relaxed and cool in his levis and white cotton jacket. His pale blue shirt lay open at the throat to reveal a glimpse of bronzed chest. He smiled across at her, his piercing green eyes exactly as she'd remembered them. Cory caught her breath, aware of a sudden warmth flooding her senses. She hadn't imagined it. There really was something akin to electricity that seemed to pass between them .

"Pardon me," she managed to say at last, her voice strained and breathless. "I didn't see you there."

"Now, that makes twice today." He feigned a frown. Straightening from his slouch, he moved out from the shelter of the narrow awning, closing the distance between them.

"Twice?"

"In the shop this afternoon. You didn't see me then either."

She hesitated, her heart beating erratically. "This desn't seem to be one of my better days," she apologized. His sudden appearance was only adding to her confusion.

"Oh?" he questioned, a twinkle in his eyes. "Am I to assume that you don't make a habit of going round causing this kind of damage?"

"Damage?"

"To my ego, of course. It's down right painful for a man to realize he's been totally unimpressive to such a pretty woman twice in one day." His voice still carried its mock seriousness.

Cory smiled. It was fortunate that he didn't know just how he had actually affected her. Even now, she felt like a melting snowball charged with static electricity. "I wouldn't say that you were totally unimpressive," she said lightly.

"Are you trying to assuage my feelings with flattery?" he taunted. "You know what they say about that."

A glint of amusement filled her eyes as she returned his unwavering stare. "It wasn't flattery, just honesty," she teased.

"Honesty, huh?" he rubbed a blunt-nailed finger across his chin, considering her words. "I'll accept that," he nodded slightly. Then he added casually, "But still, you are liable."

"I suppose you are right about that. I plead guilty to

all counts. So what is the penalty for so grievous a sin?"

"Well, for such blatant disregard for my 'amour propre,' I shall let you buy the first drink." His French slipped easily across the conversation.

Cory liked his easy banter and the warmth in his smile, but she hesitated. What did she know about this man beyond the purely physical sensations he provoked in her? Why should she trust him? He could harm her as well as anyone else.

"I promise I don't bite," he supplied, reading her too accurately. "And I'm very good at watching traffic." His face was enigmatic as he waited for her reaction.

Cory stiffened. "You saw what happened this morning?"

"You drew quite a crowd. It was lucky that your friend was so close."

Embarrassment forced a hasty explanation, "I'm quite cautious as a rule. But I guess I'm not a very good judge of these Greek drivers." She laughed nervously, trying to pass over this frightening subject.

"In Athens you must always expect the unexpected," he warned, leaning down toward her. "That's my policy, and I've yet to be proven wrong." He took her arm casually as if it were the most natural of movements. "So? What's your verdict?"

Cory stared up into the warmth of his smile, wishing her heart would beat normally again. "All right," she consented. "I'll try and make amends for my errant ways. Besides, I could use a cool drink just now. I still haven't gotten used to this heat. No wonder all of Athens sleeps at this time of day."

Cory seemed to have regained some of her lost sense of balance. She really did need something cool or at least to sit down. It must be the heat making her feel so light-headed, she thought.

"It just so happens I know of a place not far from here where they never sleep. They cater to all those crazy tourists who don't seem to mind the Greek sunshine." He smiled and directed her along the sidewalk.

It didn't surprise Cory that he'd know just where to go. "Do you know Athens well, Mr. Marcusen?"

"It's John," he supplied. "And I don't think I know Athens at all. Not even her citizens can claim that. I like to think that Athens is a mysterious woman. Seductive and beautiful, allowing you to know exactly what she wants and nothing more." He smiled down at her, a question in his jade eyes. "Wouldn't you agree, Miss Stewart?"

Cory nearly missed a step.

"In the shop this afternoon. I have to admit to doing a bit of eaves-dropping. Your friends called you Cory. Is that short for something?"

"Corinna. It was my grandmother's name."

"And did your grandmother live in Utah too?"

"Why, yes," she answered slowly. This was beginning to unnerve her. He had too many answers. "Are you psychic or something?" she challenged, trying to affect nonchallance she didn't feel.

"It's the way you talk," he supplied. "Once you hear that certain way of speaking you never quite forget."

"Do you know someone from Utah?"

"A lot of people. I'm addicted to powder skiing. I try not to let a winter pass without spending at least a week at Snowbird. Salt Lake's a beautiful city. Were you born there?"

"My parents live in one of the smaller towns outside the city. And yes, I'm a Mormon," Cory added quickly.

"For some reason that doesn't surprise me, Cory," he teased. "May I ask a personal question?"

Cory hesitated. It wasn't what she'd expected him to say. "I suppose," she consented reluctantly.

He looked at her quizzically. "Do you ever date men who aren't Mormons?"

What should she say? Was he looking for a reason to continue their acquaintance or to end it? "I don't usually ask a man his religious preferences over the dinner table," she replied a bit bruskly.

"Perhaps you should." He grinned wryly as he took her arm to lead her into a narrow side street. "You wouldn't want to fall in love with the wrong sort of guy, now would you?"

"I haven't had to worry about that lately," Cory replied without thinking.

"Much to the unhappiness of your mother, I'm sure."

Cory suddenly laughed, remembering his uncle's comment in the airport. "It seems we have something in common, Mr. Marcusen — John," she added smiling.

"It seems we have several things in common, Cory Stewart. One of them being unattached hearts." Then he joined her laughter.

About half way down there was a small cluster of tables shaded by brightly colored umbrellas, the smell of food drifting out from the open doors of a small cafe. Several couples, mostly European or American, sat around the shaded tables. John led Cory to one near the back and ordered two iced drinks. He was careful to inform her they were non-alcoholic.

"Tell me, what brought you such a long way from Salt Lake?" He settled his long form into the chair across from her.

Cory recounted briefly how she came to be invited by Edward to join this particular tour. "I wasn't too sure at first about coming, but I've had a good time, and I've seen a lot of the city." The words were out before she considered their accuracy. She'd seen the city all right, but a good time? Not unless being frightened most of the time could be considered a good time.

John seemed to sense her discomfort, steering the conversation back to a safer topic by asking about her studio at home. Cory enthusiastically responded, grateful to be on firmer ground. Their drinks were finished long before the conversation ended, but neither seemed in a hurry to leave. Cory was curious about this man. She realized, although they had talked almost non-stop since their meeting, John had revealed little of himself beyond his name. She sensed there was some direction to his questions, and he seemed to be weighing her responses carefully. It made her uneasy.

Common sense told her this was a dangerous situation for her naive heart. She was vulnerable to his easy charm. Minute by minute he was drawing her into a situation she didn't know whether she could handle or not. She'd fantasized about a dashing hero, but the reality scared her. She wanted a vacation with a happy ending, and so far nothing had gone the way she'd expected.

Cory glanced at her watch, surprised to see it was well past five o'clock. This evening's lecture on the impact of classical architecture on European Eighteenth Century decor suddenly lost much of its interest, but Cory knew she should leave this compelling man and go back to the safety of the hotel.

"Am I keeping you from something?" John's question startled her. She glanced up quickly to meet his eyes.

"You've looked at your watch twice in the last five minutes."

Cory dropped her hand to her lap. "I really must be getting back. There's a lecture scheduled for this evening, and Edward will be expecting me." She rose to go, but John captured her hand.

"Please don't go. I was hoping I could persuade you to have dinner with me. There's an excellent restaurant at the foot of Mt. Lycabettus, and the sunset view of Athens is something every tourist must see."

Cory felt the tug of his magnetic charm encircling her like a silken web. Even though she feared her heart was in danger, she heard her lips consent.

In the waning light of evening they walked down the winding path to the St. George Lycabettus Hotel where they ate roast chicken and Greek salad with fits of feta and dark hard olives. The food was delicious. Cory hadn't realized just how hungry she was. The drinks at the cafe in the city had only served to heighten her appetite. John's easy laughter and the delicious dinner eased the knot of fear in her stomach. She began to feel safer than she had at any time in the last few days.

Later, during the dessert, a sudden flash of light on the rim of her crystal goblet reminded Cory of what lay wrapped in a tissue inside her bag. The earrings . . . next to the undelivered sketch. She glanced up from the glass and caught John's eyes. He was watching her intently. "You're frowning again. Am I boring you?"

She straightened in her chair. "Sorry, I guess my mind wandered a bit. Please go on."

"It wasn't anything important. Is there something wrong?"

"Not wrong exactly, just puzzling."

"Did I tell you I'm a whiz at puzzles? Why don't you try this one on me?"

Cory laughed. "All right. You asked for it." She reached into her bag and took out the earrings. Unwrapping them carefully, she held them out for John to see. "I found these in the box that was delivered to the hotel. They came from the shop where we met this morning. I thought they were packed in my box accidentally but when I went there to return them, the man at the shop said they were purchased for me," she paused, looking at them. "He can't, or won't, tell me who sent them."

"Don't you like them?" John reached across the table and took them from her. Cory had a sudden picture of his hand holding her pencil. A shiver of warning slipped down her spine.

www.ingramcontent.com/pod-product-compliance
Lightning Source LLC
Chambersburg PA
CBHW032001240626
47153CB00003B/1067